DARK DESIRE

Titles by Emily Jane Trent

Adam & Ella
Captivated
Charmed
Cherished

Touched By You
Dark Desire
Naked Submission
The Heart's Domination
Bound By Love
Deep Obsession
Forbidden Pleasures
Raw Burn
Desperately Entwined
Fierce Possession
Intimate Secrets
Whispered Confessions
Vivid Temptation

DARK DESIRE

Touched By You 1

Emily Jane Trent

Copyright © 2013 by Emily Jane Trent.

All rights reserved. No part of this publication may be reproduced, distributed or transmitted in any form or by any means, including photocopying, recording, or other electronic or mechanical methods, without the prior written permission of the publisher, except in the case of brief quotations embodied in critical reviews and certain other noncommercial uses permitted by copyright law. For permission requests, write to the publisher, addressed "Attention: Permissions Coordinator," at the address below.

Camden Lee Press, LLC
12112 N. Rancho Vistoso Plaza Ste. 150-101
Oro Valley, AZ
www.EmilyJaneTrent.com

Publisher's Note: This is a work of fiction. Names, characters, places, and incidents are a product of the author's imagination. Locales and public names are sometimes used for atmospheric purposes. Any resemblance to actual people, living or dead, or to businesses, companies, events, institutions, or locales is completely coincidental.

Dark Desire/Emily Jane Trent. -- 1st ed.
ISBN-13: 978-1482707694
ISBN-10: 1482707691

Acknowledgements

No book is published in isolation. So many helped me, some in ways they never imagined. From my friends and family, my mentor, and a long list of indie authors, all have contributed to my success. Without my editor, cover artist, formatting expert, and others who played a part in making this book, I'd never be able to create these books for you like I do. I want to thank each of them for their good work.

A special thank you to all my readers: I've had amazing feedback on Tanner and Natalie's romantic tale. It's been very rewarding. It's my pleasure to continue to write for you. I look forward to meeting you at my fan page, Emily Jane Trent Books, or at my blog. My success is only because you read and enjoy these stories. I appreciate each of you.

Prologue

1 – Concert Night

Her upcoming graduation from high school, only weeks away, was bittersweet. She knew she'd miss her friends. They'd promised to stay in touch, but one never knew. Tonight, she was with a group that had escaped prom night for something more entertaining. Natalie had turned eighteen recently, and with senior year ending, wanted a last fling. She was so enthralled with Justin's somber voice that she didn't notice the eyes gazing at her from not far away.

Tanner Clarke had her in his direct line of vision. At the last minute, he had secured tickets to hear the group She Wants Revenge, one of his current favorites. And he could hear them just fine. He didn't need to look at them. A gorgeous young woman caught his eye and he couldn't seem to look away. He'd come alone tonight. He didn't know anyone else, personally, that liked the musical group like he did. He had to admit his taste in music was eclectic.

She looked like any other of the hundreds of women her age at the concert. She wore a short denim skirt and jacket. He couldn't see very well in the dark. Her long brown hair hung midway down her back. The soft curls begged to be touched. His seat was in the balcony and his view of her lovely, angelic face was unobstructed. He couldn't put his finger on it, but there was something special about her.

What a beauty she was, yet he noted her demeanor was unassuming. So unlike the women he was used to. He let his eyes wander, just a bit, to see if she was with a date, but no male seemed to be with her. The song ended. The little screech she let out pulled his attention back to her. She jumped up and down, clapping. Such childlike joy was foreign in his world.

The lights came up and the intermission started. Tanner slipped out to the tunnel and turned left, just in time to see her exit with a girlfriend. Figuring she'd be headed for a drink and the ladies' room, he walked in that direction, trying to keep her in sight. Hurrying a little too much, he nearly bumped into her. She stood in a line at a refreshment station, chatting with another girl her age.

Spellbound, Tanner stopped. The soft laugh she shared with her friend touched his ears and he felt it in his heart. Oh, her joy was infectious. Clearly, she was having a good time at the concert. He had no idea how to approach her. Normally, women flocked to him—whether he wanted them or not. Now, the prospect of meeting someone outside his circle of influence was a bit awkward. He wasn't really the social type.

Natalie felt someone looking at her and glanced to her left to see who it was. She found herself eye to eye with the most devastatingly gorgeous man she'd ever seen. He had to be at least six feet tall. He wore washed jeans that accentuated his lean thighs, a suede jacket that screamed high quality, and a plain white T-shirt.

But that wasn't it. There was something in his face. She couldn't think the thought she grasped for. His skin was pale and she got the impression he wasn't out in the sun much. His baby-blue eyes were so bright they appeared luminous. And his dark brown hair shimmered with auburn highlights, here under the blaring brightness of the lobby. He was just beautiful. She'd never known a man could be beautiful, but he definitely was.

"What do you want, Natalie?" Jenny's voice broke the trance. "Uh, nothing," she replied, looking away from her friend. "I'll be in the restroom." For a reason she couldn't explain, Natalie made a sudden move to get away from the captivating stranger. An unexpected feeling of desire consumed her, making her feel nervous and flustered. She couldn't imagine how she'd explain why she'd been boldly staring at him.

She had to make her escape before embarrassing herself further. Whipping around to make a dash back to the facilities, she walked directly into him, not exactly graceful. Yet he didn't seem to mind. He grabbed her arms the moment she plowed into him, and held her at arm's length, looking at her strangely. He must have stepped closer to her when she'd turned to talk to Jenny, and now blocked her path.

She wondered for a second if he was really of this world. There was no doubt that the boys she knew didn't look like he did.

Maybe it was a college look. No, that wasn't it. The expression on his face was hard to peg, as were his intentions.

He looked at her a bit harshly. "Are you in a rush to get somewhere?" he said in a deep, melodic voice. She could listen to him talk forever. But he didn't say anything else.

"Ah, I'm...um...going to the ladies' room," she stammered.

A slight smile played on his lips, but his eyes were cold. Cold, that was how they looked. That was odd. There was no reason for him to approach her and then be so rigid.

"I'll wait for you" was all he said, and then he released her. Natalie could think of no appropriate response. She turned and went straight to the ladies' room with the stranger not far behind, walked to the first stall and shut the door. Only then did she notice she was shaky. Something was happening, but she couldn't make sense of it. A gorgeous stranger just followed her to the bathroom. First of all, he was too good looking to be following her. She ran her hands down her well-worn jacket and then hugged her arms around herself in an attempt to get centered. She closed her eyes, but all she saw was the image of his face.

2– Drawn Together

Natalie walked calmly out of the restroom, fully expecting the beautiful stranger to be gone. He was more suited to being a daydream than a real person. She never met people like that. His appearance and manner gave away that he wasn't from the small area where she lived. Confidence like that was only found in the big city.

She intended to keep walking, if she could keep from tripping over her own feet, and find Jenny. She wanted to surround herself with normality and get back to the concert to get lost in the music. But such was not to be.

"Are you avoiding me?" His voice again. Her heart pounded but it wasn't fear. It felt more like excitement. Yet she had no clue how she could be excited to see someone she didn't even know. Well, on second thought, she'd have to be blind not to see that this man was a magnet for women. For the first time, a subconscious thought pressed into view. Yes, she was in trouble.

Natalie turned around and saw him standing behind her. However unlikely, he was even more handsome than she recalled. "I would never avoid someone like you." That wasn't at all what she intended to say. The words spilled out as if spoken by someone else.

The grin he gave her was blinding. Those perfect white teeth. And this time his eyes squinted when he smiled. She realized she was grinning back. Yet a tiny voice inside nagged her that he couldn't actually be interested in her. She was just an ordinary girl from Oakland, from an unremarkable neighborhood.

"I see you didn't get a chance to get a drink. The concert is going to resume shortly. I took the liberty of snagging a Coke for you, not being sure of your preference." He held out a plastic cup in offering.

Natalie felt warmth flow through her. She didn't recognize the feeling, exactly. She wasn't very experienced with men. It seemed her life was involved with more mundane activities. Yet she couldn't keep looking at him this way. Her knees were weak. "I need to sit down," she blurted out, and turned to scan for seating.

The lobby was still packed with music fans trying to get back to their seats in time. Tanner glanced at the sea of bodies and put his arm around her, guiding her along the wall to an unmarked door. Amazingly, it was unlocked. It appeared to be some kind of small lounge, possibly for employees.

Now, Natalie felt really awkward, and faint. So she plopped onto the fake leather sofa nearest the door. If she needed to make her escape, the door would be close by. "How did you know this would be open?"

Tanner looked frozen in place, a bit statue-like. It was a result of his awe over this amazing woman he was alone with. Plus, his strong features, pale skin, and stoic pose lent the impression of a perfectly carved marble statue. He'd come to this concert purposefully. So much of his life was dictated. Music was for pleasure. When he went to concerts, he liked to go alone, wanting to listen to the music without social demands. Tonight, the music was taking a backseat.

He let his eyes wander over Natalie, taking in her soft brown eyes, long brown hair, and creamy, translucent skin. His cock was hard, and had been since he'd first seen her. In the muted light of the tiny room, she looked even lovelier than she had in the balcony. He wasn't sure if she was shy or just embarrassed. Either way, she seemed nervous. He was so used to arrogant women that Natalie's humble nature touched him.

In the few seconds he stood gazing at her beauty, he battled with himself. His urges, he knew from experience, could be overpowering. The last thing he wanted was to scare away this delicate butterfly he had temporarily captured.

The silence between them was weighted. Neither knew what to do. That was unusual for Tanner. He was bold in most situations. And, really, it was bold to bring her here.

He hadn't responded to Natalie's question. He knew an answer wasn't really needed. He could have told her he knew the owner, which he did. But it didn't matter. He took two steps toward her and she stood from the seat. It seemed too natural, like some cosmic occurrence had thrown them together. Neither wanted it any other way.

Natalie was a bit out of her element. However, she was aware from his composure that this man could take the lead. And she was more than willing to have him do just that.

3 – Desire

Tanner looked at the beauty before him, standing so still. He had her alone in a private room and the thrill of that ignited his passion.

Natalie blushed, not used to being with a man in an intimate setting. Tanner's blue eyes burned into her with lust. She'd never experienced the heavy emotion that gripped her. An erotic feeling took her senses and rolled through her limb to limb. Her panties were wet and her sex tightened, embarrassingly.

In the next second, she was in his arms. Reaching out, he took her wrist and pulled her to him. She had no time to resist. Pulling her against his chest, he kissed her hard. It was a passionate kiss that sent unfamiliar emotions through her. The feel of him against her caused her to lose all sense of propriety.

Natalie's sudden desire for him surprised her. Clearly, he wanted her. One arm was around her waist, the other in her hair, tugging and clenching. His tongue found her soft, wet mouth and probed. Natalie moaned in response and slid her hot tongue along his, matching his motions.

She felt his hard cock swell against her abdomen. Excitement and nervousness coursed through her as one powerful feeling. Instinctively, she pressed into him. In response, he grabbed a handful of her long, glossy hair, pulling her head back and looking at her with a wild, predatory look.

Natalie gave a whimper when Tanner licked her neck up and down. He began to suck on her smooth skin. She felt her clit tighten when he bit her lightly, just below the jaw. She leaned her head to the side, giving him access to her sensitive neck. Taking the offer, he bit several more times along her neck, and heard her moan with pleasure.

She had her hands in his hair now, encouraging him and responding to his advances, even though all this was new to her. He licked and blew softly in her ear, melting her insides. She was panting now. He bit her earlobe and tugged it with his teeth. Natalie was at his mercy, willing him to do as he wished with her. Enraptured, she wasn't able to break free, nor did she want to.

"Baby," he whispered in a guttural voice. She gasped when he lifted her quickly in his arms and moved to the wall, pressing her back against it. He held her in his arms with her hips above his waist, and without thinking, she wrapped her legs around him. He reached under her short skirt to grab her panties. In one violent motion, he yanked them away from her body, dropping the shreds to the floor.

The sudden attack surprised her and she looked up into his eyes. He held her gaze, his hand finding her wet opening. Roughly, he ripped open her shirt and lifted one of her breasts into view, moaning deeply at the sight. His mouth found her nipple and he bit gently.

The unexpected pain that should have warned Natalie only increased her arousal. "Yes," she whimpered. All the while, she wondered at her own lack of inhibition. She was so comfortable with him, her lack of experience not seeming to matter.

Tanner freed the other creamy, round breast and swirled his tongue around the areola, sending pre-orgasmic waves through her excited pussy. Arching her back, she pressed her clit toward him, craving release. He seemed to read her mind.

With her still in his arms, he turned and placed her on a long, cushioned seat, positioning her so her legs were wide apart. Naïve though she was, Natalie was swept up in the overpowering emotion of the moment and allowed him this intimacy. She knew she should be embarrassed in this private scene, and had no idea why she was not.

Natalie, beyond even blushing, massaged her own breasts, as she had done many times when pleasuring herself. She witnessed her own brazen actions but was unable to repress her desires, such was her erotic delirium. Tanner's eyes went wide at the taboo self-touching. He leaned down to her sweet pussy, plunged his nose into her soft pubic hair, and breathed in, like an animal checking its prey. His tongue found her wetness and he stroked, tasting the hot cream between her legs.

His tongue dipped inside her moist slit. He felt his cock press against his jeans, ready to explode. Using the tip of his tongue, he touched her clit, relishing the lovely, feminine moan she rewarded him with. He held her outer lips open with his thumb and forefinger, blowing lightly on her sensitive tissue. She writhed in sensation, arching her back and pressing her naked sex upward, pleading for more. That a man could pleasure her this way amazed her.

Tanner kissed the very tip of her clit, which she felt deep within her core. He nipped her pubic area lightly, over and over, with his teeth. She felt a twinge of fear mixed with ecstasy. "Please, please," she gasped, rolling her head from side to side. Coming to her aid, he stroked his tongue along her wetness and swirled his tongue around her clit, sending convulsions of pleasure through her.

Unable to hold back, she cried out, letting the strong orgasm take her away. The release was needed and she felt gratitude for the gift of sensual pleasure. She'd never had an orgasm with a man watching her before. The idea that she was naughty only added to the titillating experience.

Tanner worked her relentlessly until the last beautiful waves stilled. Natalie was quiet, eyes closed. He reached up to stroke her cheek, admiring the flushed glow on her face. The lovely sight of her naked pussy was still exposed to him.

His cock was dripping inside his jeans and he cursed himself for not having a condom with him. He hadn't expected to need one. He leaned over, giving Natalie a slow, sensual kiss. He knew of a nearby place where he could take her. He had to be inside her. Nothing else would do. "Let's go somewhere, baby," he whispered to her.

She'd have done anything for him at that moment. "Okay," she replied, trusting him. He helped her sit up and watched her rearrange her bra and button her top. Some buttons were now lost, but the ones still there held the blouse closed—sort of. Adoringly, he smoothed her hair and helped her stand. For what seemed like an eternity to Natalie, he held her tightly in his arms. She felt so safe and happy. And very aware of his hardness pressed urgently against her.

"Okay," he said at last. "Go tell your friends I'll take you home." She nodded. "I need to know who you are," he added, holding the door closed for a moment longer.

Natalie looked at his beautiful face, lit with arousal, and marveled that he found her attractive. Next to him, she felt so average. What had just happened seemed like a dream come true. Surely, a magic spell had been cast over her.

"Natalie Baker. I live in Oakland, graduating from high school soon. This evening, I ditched prom night and came here instead; sort of a late celebration of turning eighteen." There was a moment of silence. They looked at each other, and she added with complete honesty, "I'm glad I decided to come to the concert."

His eyes gleamed with pleasure. "I'm Tanner," he said simply, and led her out the door.

4 – Abandoned

Tanner held her hand tightly. They strolled through the empty walkway, music booming through the building, locating the tunnel to Natalie's seat. Before she went to tell her girlfriend goodbye, Tanner grabbed her roughly, pulling her to him and giving her a lip-bruising kiss. Releasing her, he nodded toward the tunnel, indicating she should go.

The look in his eyes held a longing, mixed with a sternness she couldn't place. His face remained impassive, only his blue eyes gleamed—with what? The subtle change in his expression caught her attention, interrupting her state of bliss. She hesitated before turning to walk down the tunnel.

Natalie searched for her seat, her eyes slowly adjusting to the darkened concert hall. The song that had been playing when she was in the walkway dreading to leave Tanner, even for these few short minutes, had just ended. The group on stage was preparing for their next number.

She'd really looked forward to this concert. At the moment, she couldn't care less. She did hear the song echoing off the soundproofing as the music started up again. She knew the lyrics by heart from her *Save Your Soul* disc that she'd played too many times to count. The words seemed to speak to her, as they always did.

She grabbed her jacket off her seat and sat next to her friend, whispering in her ear, "I met someone."

"Who did you meet?" Her friend shot a glance toward Natalie, who was glad it was dark so she could hide the emotions racing through her.

"Tanner," she replied. "I just met him. Anyway, I've got a ride. I'll see you back home."

"Be careful," Jenny replied, and lifted her hand in a short wave before turning back to the concert.

Natalie hurried back up the tunnel, struggling to pull her jacket on as she walked. The instant she reached the light of the walkway, she looked for Tanner. Her heart raced with anticipation. At first, she didn't see him. Maybe he'd gone somewhere to sit down. But that didn't really make sense. He knew she'd be right back. Natalie walked first one direction and then the other, but the walkway was empty except for a couple of uniformed ushers.

A bolt of panic stabbed into her. Maybe he'd left. Still, she stood near the tunnel to her seat, waiting and watching. He'd appear in a minute. Time dragged by, and slowly, with much regret, she had to admit to herself that he'd vanished. The loss washed over her.

She leaned against the wall and slid to the floor. She covered her face with her hands and began sobbing. It was too much. How could she be so silly to think he'd want her? She'd never met a man like Tanner. No one had ever excited her like that, and she knew no one else ever would. But he was gone.

Emptiness clenched in her chest and the void he left threatened to drag her under. She sat there until the concert finished, when her friend found her, slumped against the wall. She got up, slowly, and left to go home. Her friend plied her with questions, but Natalie just stared blankly, with tears streaming down her cheeks and pain stabbing her heart.

Dark Desire

1 – Bittersweet

Leaving home was bittersweet for Natalie. She still couldn't believe she'd gotten into The New York Design Institute, and with the scholarship she desperately needed. There was her name at the top of the form: Natalie Christine Baker. It was really happening. She'd read the acceptance so many times the paper was tattered. She folded it and slipped it into her bag.

"Are you okay, honey?" Her mom looked at her, already knowing the truth, but needing to hear it. Emma Baker had raised her daughters alone. Nicolas Hughes had abandoned them when she was pregnant with Jazmin, who was just a year younger than Natalie. He had been tall, dark, and handsome. Emma, an incurable romantic, still loved him and felt the pain of his absence. But Nicolas hadn't married her and he'd never returned, despite her hopes.

"Yes, I'm okay Mom." Natalie felt a stab of emotional pain in her heart. Her mother was still beautiful. Jazmin and she had both inherited her brown hair, brown eyes, and clear, pale skin. At forty-seven years of age, her mom looked more like her older sister than her mother. But cirrhosis of the liver had recently developed, making her ghostly pale. She looked weak and drawn.

Her mother survived rejection from the man she fell in love with, but not without a cost. The only relief she found was in the red wine she enjoyed a little too much. She'd become an alcoholic somewhere along the way, drowning her sorrow with her poison of choice. And she was paying the price.

Natalie loved her mother dearly. Despite everything, she was a good mother. A seamstress by trade, she'd worked long, tedious hours to support her daughters. Jazmin had rejected sewing, choosing to work as a waitress instead. Natalie was not as outgoing and preferred sticking close to home. She helped with the sewing at a young age and discovered her talent for designing clothes.

Now she'd be pursuing that passion in New York, one of the world's fashion centers, so different from her hometown of Oakland, California. Excitement swelled inside her. She'd soon be in New York.

Jazmin entered the small living room, looking graceful and gorgeous, as she always did. "Ready to go?" She smiled at her older sister.

Natalie looked at her thin gold watch. "Yes, I guess we better. I don't want to miss my flight." She eyed her sister in the sleek dress she wore, one of Natalie's designs. "Jazzy, you look ravishing." She smiled. Her sister was three inches taller than Natalie. Plus, she was slender and graceful. Natalie was anything but graceful, and felt a bit too thin. But she beamed inside at her younger sister's good looks. She loved her. They'd always been close.

Emma stood, looking at her daughters with a strained look on her face. Natalie wasn't sure if it was the illness, or the fact that her oldest daughter was leaving home for the first time. With the illness, some days her mother's discomfort was worse than others. Natalie's heart wrenched at the thought. If only she could make her mother well again. But she knew that was not to be.

At least Emma had given up drinking. Physically, she just couldn't tolerate it, and both daughters kept a close eye on her. As far as Natalie knew, she'd been sober for several years now. She walked over and gave Emma a tight hug, careful not to squeeze too hard, considering her mother's frail form.

Tears formed in Emma's eyes and she dabbed them with a tissue. Natalie felt sadness press on her heart and wasn't sure she had the strength to leave. "Go now," her mother directed, conveying her support.

Natalie turned and grabbed her bag. She walked toward the car without looking back. She'd start sobbing if she looked at her mother's tearful face. Her luggage was already in the trunk. Jazzy followed her out. The future waited. Whatever it may hold for her, she was ready.

2 – New York

True to form, Jazzy chatted all the way to Oakland International Airport. Her cheerful banter did nothing to sooth the butterflies in Natalie's stomach. She'd never been to New York. Actually, she'd never been anywhere on a plane before.

The farthest she'd been was San Francisco, to eat at the restaurants or enjoy a concert. The thought of the concert where she'd had the encounter with the gorgeous stranger came to mind. Her heart pounded faster. She'd always remembered that night. She'd looked for Tanner every time she went to a concert—certain he wouldn't be there, yet hopeful. *Can you love someone you don't even know?*

He'd had an effect on her that no other man had, before or since. He seemed bold and dangerous, almost violent, which excited and confused her. Plus, he was breathtakingly gorgeous. In those few minutes they'd been together, she'd experienced a dark desire that she couldn't quell. Really, she didn't want to. Eternally, she wanted to hold the memory of that special moment of being in his arms. At least she had that.

It didn't matter that he'd disappeared. That had been four years ago, the years she'd gone to Oakland City College to save her funds for design school. Time muted the pain of the insult. She knew she wasn't his type. She was plain and very average in most ways. The only thing she had a chance of doing well was designing clothes. How could he possibly be impressed by that?

She looked over at her sister, who would be much more his type. Jazzy's thick, light brown hair fluffed out, just so. And her brown eyes had a bit of a copper tint, making them alluring. Natalie had designed clothes for years and Jazzy had been her willing model. And model she was, all five feet, nine inches of her.

"Are you excited?" Natalie realized that Jazzy was directing a question to her.

"Scared and excited, both. I don't know if I'd be able to do this without Ellis. I'm so proud of him. You know he got a job at Artisan French Cuisine, as the sous chef. He risked everything when he skipped college to go to The Culinary Institute in New York. Now it's paying off." She smiled at her friend's success.

"Yes, dear Ellis Larsen. It's a relief that he will be there for you. I'd hate to think of you going off to that big city, all by yourself. At least you know you'll eat." Jazzy giggled.

Natalie had met Ellis in high school and they'd been friends ever since. He'd given her plenty of tips on cooking. It was a great help, since she prepared the meals at home. He was always fun and they got along well.

It had never been romantic between them. Not just because Natalie never seemed interested in the boys in her hometown. It just wasn't that type of relationship.

She'd talked to him on the phone plenty since he moved to New York, where he seemed to blossom. Maybe he'd meet the right person. Certainly, he deserved it.

"And don't worry about Mom," Jazzy admonished. "I know you, big sister. You always take care of us. But I can cook. Well, maybe not like you, but we'll get by. I'll do my best."

"I know you will," Natalie agreed. "I love you, Jazzy. I'll call often, I promise."

"You'd better." She grinned.

3 – In Flight

Natalie pinched herself. The flight to New York was underway and her heart was soaring higher than the plane. Design school had always been her dream. Then the notification about the scholarship had arrived.

When she'd applied, she'd had little hope of being chosen. Apparently her designs caught someone's eye, though, and she couldn't be more grateful. She'd work hard. It wasn't work to her. She'd loved designing clothes since she was a little girl, dressing her dolls in new outfits.

Now, she had the opportunity to get her bachelor of design degree for fashion. Even with all the money she'd been able to save as a seamstress, she couldn't pay the full tuition. Without the scholarship, her education would have been delayed. She couldn't believe her luck.

The institute's brochure had proudly mentioned that some of their students had received prestigious awards from the Fashion Foundation and were awarded twelve-month internships in New York with high-profile labels such as Calvin Klein. Natalie pushed the idea aside for now. It was enough that she'd be in the program. She couldn't be greedy. But she'd sure give it her best when the time came.

Out of the small window of the plane she could only see clouds. She put her head back and closed her eyes. There he was—Mr. Gorgeous, tall and lean, his pale skin contrasting against his dark brown hair with brilliant auburn highlights. She could still feel his rock-hard muscles, smell his male scent, and hear his baritone voice, just as though she were in his arms.

She felt the pressure of his swollen cock against her and the erotic feel of his tongue every time she masturbated. She'd never be able to explain why, after such a long time, he appeared in her mind frequently, or why the memory was so vivid. The image was burned in her mind. She should have dated more. Now, the memory of that night was all she had.

She couldn't delude herself. What she felt

was strong, very strong. It seemed nothing could erase her desire for him, nor did she want it to. Just the opposite—she clung to her desire like a lifeline. There he was, emblazoned in her fantasies, his stern countenance in conflict with his gleaming baby-blue eyes. If she could paint a picture of the perfect man, it would be him—Tanner. She'd often said his name out loud when no one was around to hear her.

It wasn't that she had never been asked on a date. She just never felt that kind of attraction to any other man. All others, frankly, seemed inadequate compared to Tanner's feral, rough sexuality. She guessed she was weird. All her friends dated.

Her mother encouraged her to go out more, reassuring her that she didn't need to be home so much. Maybe her mother feared that her own nightmare-like relationship with an irresponsible man had jaded Natalie. But it was really the opposite. Natalie admired her mother's undying love for one man, no matter that it was ill placed.

She often wondered where Tanner was and what he was doing, even though she had no right to care. Surely, by now, he was married. He was several years older than she was. From the look of him, he'd probably attended some Ivy League school. Odd she remembered his upper-class look. Well, not really. She remembered everything about him, as if time could not erase the images.

Here she was, leaving home for the first time at age twenty-two. She wondered if he ever thought about her. She shook herself back to reality. Sometimes, Tanner seemed more real than her normal life. She'd have to watch that. He didn't even know she existed.

The idea that he even remembered what happened at the concert was remote. She envisioned he had a very full, successful life—wherever he was. She'd known from the start that he was in a different class than she. At best, she was a tiny speck in his past. And that was enough for her; just the memory that she'd been with him, for a brief moment in time, meant everything.

4 – Ellis

Flying into LaGuardia Airport was quite an experience for a girl who'd rarely been outside rural America. Natalie had purposely taken an early flight, so it would still be light when she landed. There was no way she'd fly in after dark and miss seeing the Statue of Liberty.

There was the lady of freedom, standing tall against the flat ocean. The landing was too quick to suit Natalie. She wanted a longer look at the statue from above. At least she saw the beautiful symbol of freedom, as not every landing offered that view. It depended on the approach taken to the landing strip. She felt lucky. Maybe New York would mean good things for her.

Inside the terminal was bedlam. She'd never seen so many people in one place and was relieved to see her friend's smiling face. At over six feet tall, he stood above the crowd and was not far from her. She saw his pale blue eyes, light brown hair, and handsome face. "Ellis!" she shouted. The noise level prevented him from hearing her.

But Ellis was looking at each person as they exited and spotted Natalie even before she yelled. "Natty!" He strode forward and wrapped his arms around her for a tight hug. She giggled with delight, all concern and fear of the new city dissipated by his familiar presence. She hadn't seen him since he'd moved to New York, but they chatted frequently by cell phone or annoyed each other with endless texting.

Ellis got Natalie efficiently through baggage claim and safely into his silver Volkswagen GTI. They both stopped for a breath before continuing. "Nice car," she said, looking around.

"I like it. It's the sporty model." He beamed at her. "I take the subway most of the time, though."

"It's so great to see you," she said. "Let's get out of this airport. I'm getting claustrophobic."

"Sure thing. How about some food? I know they don't feed you on those flights. As a chef, the idea of bagged peanuts is revolting."

"Actually, I'm starved." She sighed, rubbing her belly.

Dinner was at a quiet place that Ellis frequented, if you could call anywhere in New York quiet. All the way to Gino's Trattoria, Natalie looked out the window, drinking in the sights. The little Italian restaurant was everything Ellis promised. It was cozy and the food was excellent. They shared a bottle of Nebbiolo, an Italian red that Ellis chose. She dug into her spaghetti with meatballs and caught up on news between bites.

Natalie listened while Ellis filled her in on the restaurant where he'd been hired. It served French cuisine and he was fortunate enough to work with a world-renowned chef. He hadn't met anyone special yet in his personal life. Now that he was out of culinary school, he'd have more time to socialize. He was just so glad to see her, and she felt exactly the same.

Their time together seemed to speed by. He dropped her off at the home of Cheryl Easton, an instructor at the design institute she'd be attending. She was renting a room. She felt fortunate to have found something affordable.

During admissions, students were

provided with assistance to locate lodgings. Paying for a room in Cheryl's home, not far from the institute, was perfect. Natalie wasn't sure why Cheryl wanted to rent space in her lovely penthouse, near the Fashion District, and for such a reasonable price. But she was thrilled that she did.

Cheryl Easton was a former fashion model. Natalie was looking forward to meeting her. She had connections in the industry and made some guest appearances at the institute. From the photos Natalie had seen of the penthouse, Cheryl lived a luxurious lifestyle.

Parking was impossible, so Ellis let Natalie out of the car in front of the building. On the way over she'd called, so Cheryl was expecting her and buzzed her up immediately.

5 – Cheryl's Penthouse

Cheryl Easton was more striking in person than in her photos. She looked much younger than her forty-eight years. She was several inches taller than Natalie and seemed to glide when she walked, such was her grace, achieved from years on the runway. Natalie tried not to embarrass herself by tripping over her own feet.

"Hello, Cheryl. I'm Natalie. It's so good to be here," Natalie managed to state without becoming tongue-tied in front of the famous model and sex symbol, but found she was staring. Cheryl's brown eyes had a bronze hue and were the most unique color Natalie had ever seen. Her long, dark hair hung far below her shoulders. Her short bangs contrasted with the dramatic length.

"Welcome," Cheryl greeted her warmly.

"Let me show you to your room first. We can chat and get to know each other once you get settled." Cheryl strode ahead, her long, slender legs showing beneath the short, tight skirt and her radiant black hair blowing around her as if she'd be photo-ready at a moment's notice.

Natalie's rented room looked like something out of a magazine. It was a corner bedroom with deep magenta carpet. Otherwise, everything was white, including the walls, the bed cover, the four posts of the bed, and the sheer canopy. The contrast was stark. Two of the walls were floor-to-ceiling windows with breathtaking views of the high rises in the Upper East Side. Natalie walked to the window and looked out at the massive city.

If only Jazzy were here with me, she wished, as she dialed her cell phone. "Jazzy, I'm here," she told her. "It's unbelievable! You should see the view from my bedroom."

"Oh, Natty, it's so good to know you got there safely. I wish I could see it. Maybe I can visit sometime," Jazzy replied.

"Yes, I'll make sure you do," Natalie assured her. "Everything okay there?"

"Yep, all is well. Mom misses you but I'm taking good care of her. She's been tired today, just all the excitement of seeing you off, I think. Right now, she's sleeping. I'll tell her you arrived safely. We can talk again tomorrow night. I want to hear all about what it's like there," Jazzy said.

"Absolutely," Natalie agreed. After hanging up, she did a quick unpack and went out to the main room, to get to know Cheryl.

Cheryl was very interested in Natalie, her family, her career, and who she knew in New York. Natalie told her about Ellis, her friend from home who worked as a chef. But other than him, Cheryl was the only person she knew so far. She told her about her sister and her mother, and how much she missed them already.

Natalie gushed with enthusiasm about finally making it to New York to attend design school. It meant so much to her. But what she wanted to hear about was Cheryl and all about the fashion world.

Natalie was enthralled, chatting with Cheryl like they'd been girlfriends for years. Cheryl was not only a stunning woman of the world, but exhibited a warm, friendly personality as well. "Modeling is an exciting career, but it's not for every woman. Those of us who do succeed start with the right body type, but it takes hard work to be a supermodel.

"I think back on it, and realize I could only do that when I was young. My diet was very strict. Prior to a big show, especially if the clothing was revealing, I'd only drink protein shakes, no solid food at all. Plus, I drank a lot of water so I wouldn't bloat. Then, hours before the show, I wouldn't drink at all, so I could drop several pounds.

"Like peaking for any sport, it takes dedication. And the schedule can be grueling. But I wouldn't trade it for anything. I had the opportunity to wear many expensive designs. I met so many interesting, talented people, and got to travel. It was a time to remember.

"But I'm glad that I don't have to maintain such a strict diet, or work out twice a day anymore." Cheryl smiled pleasantly. "I model a bit, still. And I enjoy being a guest instructor at the design school. The passion of the new designers is very inspiring."

Natalie couldn't take her eyes off the lovely woman. She was still as slender as a reed and stunningly beautiful. As far as she could tell, a more relaxed diet and exercise program had done nothing to detract from

Cheryl's image.

"I'm glad I design the clothes instead of wear them," Natalie confessed. "I'm not graceful enough to stride along those runways in front of crowds, or even in front of millions of people, like the fashion shows you see that are broadcasted."

Cheryl's eyes gleamed with amusement. "Oh, you'd be surprised. You could learn all that. But I'm sure you're more valuable designing the outfits. I'm looking forward to seeing more of your work. I did see the samples you sent to the school. You have a fresh take on design. I'd say you have a lot of promise."

Natalie was embarrassed at the flattery. She'd only designed clothes at home and had yet to be tested in the high-fashion atmosphere. "Thank you." She blushed. "I hope you're right."

6 – Madison Avenue

Madison Avenue was everything she expected and more. All the buildings were crammed together, skyscrapers blotting out the sky. Natalie looked up at the tops of the buildings, bending her neck until it hurt, looking up at the view. She'd heard the scene described as concrete canyons with inimitable skylines, and it was exactly that.

She couldn't wait to see Madison Square Garden and other sights not far away. She'd have plenty of opportunity, since the program at the design institute didn't start for weeks. She'd arrived early to allow time to adjust to the big city and do some long-anticipated sightseeing. She'd also be working part time as a seamstress at the design school and wanted to get grooved in before starting her studies.

For now, she was focused on New York's

haute couture, the small shops selling fabulous clothes with price tags she couldn't begin to afford. But she could look. Just the thrill of being here had her grinning. She'd taken a cab this first day, knowing she'd need to get used to the subway, but putting it off. It was overwhelming enough to absorb all the activity around her.

She'd have to spend more time here, visiting the designer labels: Dolce & Gabbana, Ralph Lauren—well, too many to mention. And there was Barney's, a huge department store. She could get lost there for weeks and likely would do just that.

For now, Davi Designs was the one she spotted. The shop was smaller than the more well-known shops and housed designs from Brazilian designer Davi Carvalho, a new rising star in the fashion world. New York was the designer's first location outside of Brazil, she'd learned. Knowing Natalie was intent on seeing Madison Avenue today, Cheryl had suggested she stop in.

Natalie's eyes went big when she entered. Seeing fashions in magazines was not the same as this. She was glad she'd worn one of her own designs today, feeling otherwise out of place. At least she could be proud of what she was wearing. No one else would know that she'd sewn a temporary hem so it would fit her. Her designs were scaled for a model much taller than she was.

If only she'd had time to do something more with her hair. It hung to mid-back, her long brown curls held on one side with a tortoiseshell clip.

She took a deep breath before going further. She'd have to get herself together if she planned to live in New York and be part of the fashion world. At the counter was a tall, thin blonde with impeccable makeup and glittering bracelets. It was a dazzling image. The sales clerk looked like a movie star.

She stepped forward to browse the fashions, but her shoe slipped on the polished floor. She lost her balance for a moment. Not a great first impression. She casually flipped her long hair over her shoulder and reached for a dress on the rack, appearing to be a normal customer, she hoped.

A strong, deep, male voice echoed in the small shop. The domineering tone shocked her. She hadn't seen anyone else a moment ago. And the voice seemed familiar. But how could that be? She didn't know anyone in New York yet.

Out of the corner of her eye, she risked a glance, not wanting to stare. No, it couldn't be! She would never forget him, ever. It was him, the gorgeous hunk from the concert—Tanner.

Tanner! Here? She blushed, even though she was hidden behind other racks of clothing, or so she thought.

"I'll need to see it modeled," she heard him say. "I cannot tell how it will flow when it's just on a hanger." Even from a distance, she could see that the blonde was caught, not knowing how to resolve the issue. A moment of silence was followed by muffled talking. He was whispering something.

Natalie couldn't pull her attention away. It was him. He was really here. Her feet were frozen to the floor. She had the urge to dash out of the store, having no idea what she would say to Tanner, or how to react after all this time. And she couldn't just continue shopping. He'd spot her for sure.

The decision was made for her. "Excuse me, miss." The blond clerk had materialized beside her. "This is a bit unusual, but the gentleman has asked for a favor. Would you mind putting on this dress and modeling it? He'd just like to see it on a real woman before making a decision."

Natalie's heart raced. Modeling the dress for him seemed as unlikely as, well, being here in New York in the Fashion District. Maybe they did that kind of stuff here. She started to shake her head, declining the request, just out of self-preservation.

Graceful she was not. There was no way she could stroll around in that dress in front of him. As it was, she was shaking and barely able to continue standing. She realized she was in shock.

"I...ah" was as far as she got.

The blonde leaned in closer to whisper, "Please, it won't take long. You may not recognize who that is...he leads a very private life. But that's Steven Tanner Clarke. He inherited Clarke Luxury Brands from his father. You may have heard of William Sheldon Clarke?"

Natalie didn't say a word. The mention of Clarke Luxury Brands had been like cold water on her face. If Tanner owned the company now, he was one of the richest people in the world and his company was influential in the fashion world, the world she intended to join.

She was trapped. She had no choice but to model the dress. The last thing she wanted to do was insult such a powerful man. One word from him could wipe out her chances of a career in fashion design. Timidly, she reached out and took the hanger in her hand. "The dressing room?" she asked in a nervous voice.

7 – Modeling

Natalie began making her way to the dressing room. She found the nerve to look up and was eye to eye with him, his piercing blue eyes watching her every move. Her heart thudded at the thought he might recognize her, but she couldn't imagine he'd remember after so many years. Plus, she looked different—more mature, she hoped.

If only she could make it to the dressing room without incident. Feeling shy, she looked down to avoid his gaze, when what she really wanted was to look at him for the rest of her life.

She could smell his expensive cologne as she walked by where he was standing, smiling. There was a look of recognition, or was it her imagination? She couldn't find her voice, so just gave a short nod as she passed him and found a momentary haven in the elaborate dressing room.

She shut the door and leaned against the wall with her eyes closed. "Let me know if you need any help." The clerk had been following a few steps behind her.

The kind of help I need you won't be able to provide, she thought, but only said, "All right."

Tanner was on the other side of the thin door she leaned against. He was there, in the flesh. Her memories clashed with reality, leaving her weak and slightly faint. She tried to push the past away, but her body betrayed her. The thin satin panties she wore were wet and her clit was hard. The heat that flooded through her was palpable, and she had no idea how she'd hide it from Tanner's view.

Natalie took a deep breath and opened her eyes to examine the dress. *I can do this*. It was a short black evening dress, with lace at the low-cut bodice and around the waist. Checking the price tag, she let out an involuntary gasp. This would be the most expensive dress she'd ever touched, much less worn. The clerk knocked softly and handed Natalie a flesh-colored strapless bra and some black heels.

The dress fit her, the black satin hugging

her feminine curves. She wished for a moment that Jazzy were with her. She always made such a good model. But Natalie was alone. Before stepping out, she rearranged her hair with the wide clip, holding most of it up at the back. A few tendrils hung free. That would have to do.

The shoes were a bit wide, allowing her foot to slide around. At least the heels weren't too high. Maybe she had a prayer of pulling this off without revealing her lack of grace. She added a touch of the crimson lipstick she'd carried in her purse, left the purse in the room, and exited in her best posture, imitating confidence. She walked carefully, one step at a time, out of the dressing room, and reentered the shop.

Natalie consciously pushed thoughts of her erotic encounter with Tanner out of her mind. She needed to put her dream world behind her and focus on the present. Anxiously, she wondered if she could stay focused on anything but Tanner, especially with him so close that his male pheromones were making her swoon.

Tanner was pacing back and forth. It stuck Natalie that he appeared impatient, almost short-tempered, which seemed out of place in these circumstances.

He noticed her standing there in the dress and his heart surged. She was so beautiful. Nothing about her was fake or pretentious. She was a natural beauty. The way she stood there, so shy, he wondered if she had any idea how stunning she was. His cock, already swollen from his first sight of her, pressed against his pants.

"Please," he directed in an unwavering tone. "Come on out. I'd like to see you walk around, if you don't mind." He watched her walk.

A bit of cleavage showed at the top of the dress and Tanner could feel the warmth of her breasts when she passed within inches of where he stood, gawking. He could see her nipples outlined under the thin garments. He watched her stroll by, her slender hips swaying under the satin fabric. His imagination began to run wild.

Natalie was glad the shoes had a soft rubber sole, because the last thing she wanted was to go sliding across the polished wood floor. With shoulders back and head up, she made her best effort at showing off the dress. That was what he wanted to see, after all. Yet the idea that he might recognize her nagged without reprieve.

She walked up to the front door of the

shop, turned, and walked back to where Tanner waited. She was just about to breathe a sigh of relief when she wobbled in the leather heels. Trying to regain her balance was fruitless. She felt herself falling with nothing nearby to grab on to.

So fast that she didn't see him move, Tanner was at her side. He blocked her fall very gallantly and stood, like a solid wall of masculine muscle, with his arm around her waist. Natalie felt her insides turn to mush. Fortunately, she hadn't fallen, thanks to his smooth rescue. But being this close to him again melted her.

He smelled so good, fresh and of men's cologne. His strength was impressive. He looked lean and was hard as a rock. She felt like a feather in his arms. Bringing herself back to the matter at hand, she stood on her own feet and smoothed the skirt of the dress. Being practical and done showing off, she reached down to remove the offending heels.

Tanner stood without moving a muscle, gazing lustfully at her. He wanted to lift her in his arms and... "No," he said aloud.

Natalie looked at him. "What?"

"I mean...are you okay?" he asked.

"Yes, thank you." Natalie took a step

toward the dressing room while lifting the black heels she held in her hand, indicating she had no intention of walking in them again. "Just to be safe," she said as she gestured and managed a smile. And Tanner smiled back.

8 – Lunch

Natalie looked at Tanner, standing alone at the counter. The blond clerk was busy with something in back.

"Thank you. The dress looked magnificent. I'll have it delivered," he told her, his face impassive. The price flashed in her mind, but then he could surely afford to buy whatever he wanted. He could buy the whole shop.

"Well, thank you for saving me. I'll never understand how runway models do it, walking in those shoes. I'd kill myself." She gave a little laugh. The soft laugh caressed Tanner, touching him the same as her hand on his cheek would have. It gave him a feeling of happiness that was foreign to him. He couldn't get this close and lose her again.

"I'm taking you to lunch," he said,

definitively. It was more of a command than a request. All the reasons to decline evaporated as quickly as Natalie thought of them. She wanted to be with Tanner, more than anything. He'd be shocked to know she'd thought of him every day since she'd met him.

She tried to conceal her joy at the invitation. "I'd be delighted, sir," she replied.

Tanner didn't miss the gleam in her eyes. He moved to stand beside her, placing his arm under hers in a chivalrous manner and giving a quick, at-your-service bow, said politely, "Shall we?" And with that, he guided her out of the shop.

The Rosewood Hotel was elegant. Tanner seemed completely at home. Inside, he escorted her to the Carlyle Restaurant and they were seated in a small dining room, off the main room. The décor reminded her of an English manor, and there were paintings of hunting scenes adorning the walls.

Tanner didn't miss a beat, noticing that Natalie was feeling lost. "What would you like to eat?" he asked.

The menu items were so pricey she had no idea what to order. She rolled her shoulders, conveying her confusion. Tanner inquired, "Do you prefer seafood, beef, or are you vegetarian?"

"Seafood," she answered with conviction.

"Excellent, then we'll have the seafood salad. It's delicious." Decision made.

Natalie didn't feel very hungry. Being in such an elegant restaurant with Tanner, she felt like she had stepped into another world. She never wanted lunch to end, knowing she'd likely never see him again. It occurred to her that he'd never asked her name. However, the sales clerk had told her about him and, for the first time, she knew his full name.

Natalie made an effort to calm her nerves. Tanner had such an effect on her that she had to make a point to breathe or she'd hold her breath, unconsciously. She let Tanner manage the lunch orders. It was too much for her. As long as she could sit here and watch him, she was happy.

Tanner ordered light champagne to start the meal, which was served with crusty French bread and herbed butter. The waiters wore formal attire—white shirts with black pants—and the service was impeccable. How Natalie noticed this she wasn't sure, because she didn't take her eyes off the handsome sight in front of her.

She didn't want to miss even a minute of her time with him.

She'd dreamed of him ever since that very first encounter. She could hear his voice, smell his skin, and feel his heat. It was imagination, but nonetheless vivid. And now he was with her. He'd invited her to lunch without even asking her name. If someone shook her to wake her from this dream, it wouldn't surprise her.

9 – Revelation

Natalie had to admit that Tanner was even more gorgeous in person than in her memory. Maybe he'd matured. It looked good on him. She couldn't imagine anything that wouldn't look good on him. If a photographer stepped in and snapped a photo of Tanner for a magazine cover, it would be quite appropriate.

He was long and lean, like she remembered. Her face heated at the recent feel of him against her. He was solid, like beautiful, smooth stone. His skin was pale against his dark hair, and even in the low restaurant lights, she could see the shimmery auburn highlights causing the light to glitter off him. Yes, glitter, she thought. He glittered.

He was dressed for business in a charcoal gray pinstripe suit, accented with a white shirt, crisply starched, and a blue satin tie that matched the color of his eyes. He was luscious. The cufflinks looked expensive. Just as she thought when she met him years ago, he was all class.

She blushed as she realized she was staring at him and he was suppressing a little smile, but his eyes gleamed. She quickly took a sip of her champagne, not wanting to embarrass herself.

"You're blushing," he commented. He had a sly look and Natalie wondered what was going through his mind, but she didn't have to wonder long.

"You remember me, don't you?" he asked bluntly, and her face reddened. He did know!

"You're hard to forget," she replied, looking down to hide her reaction.

"So are you," he said flatly. Natalie looked up instantly. She wasn't clear about what he meant. Was it possible that he remembered her, like she did him? No, that would be too much to hope for.

She looked at him blankly. Tanner's eyes turned a darker blue, intensifying his look. "You're beautiful when you blush," he told her without hesitation. Her blushing and nervousness was turning him on. Her behavior begged for his control. And he did like women he could control.

Natalie's mind raced. She couldn't be sure how much he remembered. Surely the memory wasn't the same for him as for her. And now, by chance, they'd met again. She needed to keep her cool. She didn't want to appear a simpering, needy woman. She didn't know a lot about men, considering her lack of experience. But she guessed men didn't like clinging women.

"I'm blushing because you're being very cryptic. What is it I should remember about you?" Her chin lifted in a challenge. Her tactic was to let him show his cards first. Otherwise, she might overstep polite conversation and leap into his arms. Oh, how she'd wanted to, for so long.

Tanner's voice was softer and he leaned in, closer to her. "I've never forgotten you, since that night at the concert."

Natalie flushed with desire. If only he really meant that. Then it occurred to her that he'd disappeared on her that night. She should be upset with him, although she'd never been able to maintain her rightful level of anger. Really, she felt more loss, like an irreparable heartbreak. She didn't dare reveal that.

"Well, you seemed to forget me pretty easily. You vanished and I never heard from you again," she blustered, hoping she sounded mean enough.

"I'd like to offer my apology," he said sincerely. "There is an explanation, but I don't want our first lunch together to be about my failings. Given I have plenty. But I'd rather focus on you."

Natalie was caught off guard. He looked at her without blinking, looking so handsome. He was being honest, as best she could tell. However, she couldn't fathom what failings he could mean. He was perfect. If she knew nothing else, she knew that. And that night, even though he had abandoned her, there was a kindness about him that had instantly affected her. She'd never been able to hate him for the betrayal.

"Okay, I accept your apology," she said, and her heart swelled. She couldn't look at him, with that pleading face, and not give in. He had her wrapped around his little finger. That had been the case since she'd first caught him looking at her with those baby-blue eyes. That moment, standing in line to get a Coke during the concert intermission, had changed her life. Only now was she beginning to realize how much.

"That's better." he smiled briefly and leaned back in his chair. She was enough to make him want to lose all control, and *that* he couldn't allow. He drank in her beauty. Her long curls, her wide brown eyes, and her delicate, pale skin gave her an unearthly beauty. He so wanted to kiss that lovely, feminine mouth, the most perfect mouth he'd ever seen. He remembered her sweet, innocent kiss and wanted more, much more.

10 – Becoming Friends

Natalie found herself uncommonly relaxed with Tanner. She noticed that she answered everything he asked with utter honesty. That was unusual. She tended to be a little shy and rarely revealed her inner feelings, especially with men.

She talked on and on about her hopes as a dress designer and her chance to finally attend the design institute. Even how she'd learned to sew as a little girl and helped her mother, who was a seamstress by trade. Her creative designs were proudly worn by her younger sister, but so far no one else had discovered them. She intended to change that.

"I marvel at your passion. I've worked with many designers. Those with passion are the only ones with a chance of success. The business is too competitive. You have to be tough and determined to make it." His face revealed no emotion.

"So, you inherited the business from your father?" she asked, very intrigued.

"Yes, he groomed me for this business since I was a young boy. He always intended for me to take over some day. Unfortunately, that day came sooner than either of us planned. He had an undiagnosed heart condition and, two years ago, he died of a sudden heart attack."

Natalie saw darkness come over Tanner. He went more rigid and appeared stern, but she wouldn't have labeled it sadness or grief. She regretted asking such a personal question so soon. "I'm so sorry," she said.

"He was a good businessman and had systems in place. He'd done a good job of training and interning me. Ideally it would have been longer, but it was sufficient," Tanner continued. He loved his father, but he'd never had the luxury of experiencing grief over his death. He'd cried privately after the funeral. But to all appearances, he was a tower of strength.

"Clarke Luxury Brands includes many of the top designers, right?" Natalie hoped she wasn't prying, but fashion design, in any form, had her interest. And she wanted to know everything she could about Tanner. He was spellbindingly gorgeous and struck her as strong, both physically and emotionally.

For some reason, she found herself strongly attracted to his stern, powerful countenance. Men aren't supposed to cry, she guessed. She'd heard that, but never had a close male relationship, so was all the more curious about Tanner's personality.

"Yes, many of the top fashion designers fall under our business umbrella. But we also have companies that include fine jewelry, handbags, and highly rated wines and champagnes," he explained.

Natalie held up her flute before taking another sip of the exquisite, bubbly liquid and asked, "One of yours?" Tanner nodded, but appeared unaffected by the notion. Natalie supposed it was a familiar occurrence for him, no matter how special it seemed to her.

Tanner quickly tired of talking about himself. It was business, and he was grateful to his father. There was no doubt that he'd continue the family tradition. Being one of the wealthiest men in the world had many advantages. Tanner valued his position and worked hard to expand the wealth so generously bequeathed to him.

Right now, he was interested in only one thing—Natalie. She'd slipped through his hands once before. He'd no intention of letting that happen again.

The nagging thought that he should leave her alone lost power over him the more he was with her. The magnetism he felt was not going to be so easily ignored. Maybe once, when they'd lived in different states, he could have let her life unfold as if he'd never appeared, but not now.

They were together in New York, and the urges that gripped Tanner from deep inside were overpowering. He faced the fact that he'd never be able to walk out of this restaurant and just leave her alone, even though he should.

He'd left the night of the concert, so many years ago. He hadn't wanted to hurt her. She was so lovely and naïve and he'd been drawn to her without warning. Leaving that first night was a clear message that he wouldn't be good for her. Yet she didn't seem to hold it against him. Nor did she seem afraid of him. Quite the opposite—she was comfortable in his presence, which wasn't what he expected.

Tanner reflected on the women he'd been

with sexually. He needed sex and was clear on his preferences. He wasn't sure if Natalie would surrender to him and his demands. He didn't want to mar her innocence, but his need was becoming paramount.

11 – The Invitation

Natalie looked at Tanner with pure admiration. He was beautifully sculpted, a male form that statues of Adonis were modeled after. And he was capable, intelligent, and unfathomably wealthy. What woman in her right mind wouldn't want him? And she'd felt all-consuming emotion the first moment she'd seen him, before she even knew his name. There was something special about this man.

The delicious food had come and gone. Dessert had been offered and declined. It was time to part. The pain in Natalie's heart was agonizing. If only she could hold him in her arms, like she did that night so long ago.

"I want to see you again," Tanner stated. The uncertain look on his face almost made her giggle. That was a question he didn't really have to ask, but then he didn't know that yet. Did he really think she'd refuse?

"I'd love to," she replied, her heart pounding so loudly she feared he could hear it.

"It's short notice, but there is a fashion show tomorrow afternoon that I think you'd be particularly interested in. From what you tell me of your designs, you'll find it inspiring," he said. "I'd like for you to attend with me, if you don't have other plans."

Natalie's heart fluttered and she felt giddy, but she did her best to sound relaxed. She didn't want to blow it. So far, things seemed to be going okay. She crossed her fingers under the table for luck. It was the only thing she could think to do that would calm her.

"I'd be pleased to attend," she agreed.

"I'll pick you up at two, tomorrow," he said.

"That will be fine. I'm staying with Cheryl Easton in the Upper East Side. She's been kind enough to allow me to stay with her," she told him. Cheryl was famous worldwide in fashion and she had no doubt that Tanner would know her.

"Yes, I've been to her place," Tanner replied.

"Oh." Natalie didn't know that they knew each other that well, although it would make sense. Possibly the world of fashion was a close-knit community. "Okay then, that will be fine."

12 – *Dreams*

Tanner had a meeting to attend. He'd offered to have his driver take Natalie wherever she needed to go, but she'd assured him that she had other business on Madison Avenue. He'd reluctantly let her walk out of the restaurant, his protective nature urging him to see her safely escorted.

This early in the relationship, he couldn't really argue with her. She'd lived on her own until now. For the present, he'd have to let her continue to do so, despite wishing otherwise. She seemed a little anxious to escape his presence. He didn't think he'd come on too strong. But he wasn't the best judge of that.

Throughout lunch, he'd been hard and achy for her. He'd found the inner restraint to hold back, even though she had a profound effect on him. She always had.

She was a beautiful dream, a dream he hoped to never stop having. He'd given her years away from him. Time and again, he'd wanted to fly back to find her and see her. It was good there had been so much distance between them. If she'd been closer, he'd never have been able to deny his desire.

He knew he wasn't good for her. He'd almost hoped she had a boyfriend, an excuse he couldn't sweep aside. All through lunch, she'd only talked about her mother and her sister. If there was another love in her life, surely she would have mentioned him.

And now, she was so close. He'd smelled her sweet aroma when he'd prevented her fall in the shop, when he'd moved closer to talk to her and when she'd stood near him to say goodbye, thanking him for lunch. She drove him crazy, inciting a flame of desire that would burn them both if he wasn't careful.

If he didn't have that meeting to go to, he'd be at home, relieving his aching balls. There was always his private lounge. Yes, he'd lock the door and masturbate, thinking of her. It certainly wouldn't be the first time.

Natalie couldn't fathom the depths of her

emotion for Tanner. Every time she was with him, she didn't want their time together to end. He'd said she was beautiful. She kept replaying his words in her head. How nice it sounded. She was so glad he thought so, or at least was nice enough to say so. She felt plain next to his extraordinary looks. When she dressed up, she could be very presentable, but never considered herself beautiful like her sister.

Her sweet sister was never vain, so didn't rub it in. But once in a while, Natalie wished she'd grown three more inches, so she could be long and slender like her. As it was, she felt a bit too slim. With all the stress of taking care of the family and working and planning for New York, she'd lost a couple of pounds and her clothes fit looser. She'd have to work on that. At home, she'd always stayed in shape. She was glad to hear that Cheryl's building had a fitness center. It suddenly became important for her to look good for Tanner.

She giggled to herself about Tanner inviting her to the fashion show. The knowledge she'd see him at least one more time was comforting. He roused a feeling in her that no one else had. Through the last four years of college, she'd been asked out sometimes. It always surprised her when a man showed interest. But she if hadn't felt the same, she didn't see the point of going on a date and having to pretend. Being fake wasn't something she could do well. She was direct and honest to a fault.

She knew there would never be anyone but Tanner. How odd that she'd never faced that fact. But seeing him again, feeling the strength of desire he aroused, she knew he was the only one for her. It was really too bad, because she wasn't good enough for him. But she tried to convince herself that she'd cherish her moments with him, and that would have to be enough.

13 – The Dress

After lunch the day before, Natalie hadn't wasted a moment before calling Jazzy to tell her about the day's events. She spoke to her mother first, assuring herself that her mother was feeling as well as could be expected. Emma was tired, as she usually was, but stable. "Nothing to be concerned about," her mom assured her. She was very sweet and so happy for Natalie. The conversation warmed Natalie's heart.

Jazzy got back on the line and Natalie gushed about modeling the dress and being taken to lunch, describing the restaurant experience in great detail. She omitted the part about knowing Tanner earlier, or what had happened at the concert so many years before. She wanted to tell her. It was just hard to explain, especially over the phone.

Natalie was having trouble deciding what

to wear. She'd never been to a New York fashion show, and her wardrobe wasn't up to those standards. She considered wearing one of her own designs that she'd brought with her. She stood in front of the mirror and held them up one at a time. The trouble was all the dresses were made for Jazzy, who was taller and slightly fuller.

The buzzer sounded and Cheryl answered to receive a package for her new houseguest. She buzzed the deliveryman into the building.

"Natalie, there's a package for you," she called, and walked toward the hall. Natalie couldn't imagine what it was, unable to think of anything her sister would send her. She wasn't aware of forgetting anything important when she'd packed for New York. And if she had, Jazzy would have mentioned it. After all, they talked every day.

Natalie looked at Cheryl, reading the pleasure in her face. Cheryl wore a royal blue velvet jumpsuit, having just returned from a jog. *She'd look stunning in jeans with holes in them,* Natalie mused. Taking the box, she walked to the front room and sat on one of the embroidered chairs. She ripped the brown paper off, noticing who the sender was. It was printed boldly as the return address.

She hadn't ordered anything... *Oh*. She just sat there and looked at the dress. It must be a mistake, she thought. Taking it out, she stood and held it to her. Giving a little laugh, she looked over at Cheryl. "What do you think?"

"It was made with you in mind." Cheryl grinned, showing her perfect, white smile. "Who is it from?"

Natalie took the small envelope from inside the box and ripped it open. A note was written in bold, masculine script: *The dress looked lovely on you. I'd love to see you in it again this afternoon — Tanner*

Putting her hand over her heart, Natalie sighed. "Tanner sent it to me. Remember, I told you last night that he asked me to model it for him yesterday when I happened to be in the same shop. He wanted to see what it looked like, other than on the rack.

"And now he's sent it to me. Wants me to wear it to the fashion show," Natalie told her attentive roommate. "But it's so expensive. I'll be very careful with it and return it, right after the event."

"No, you won't," Cheryl said sharply.

"Never return a man's gift. It would be an insult. He wants you to have the dress. That's why he sent it. Give him the pleasure he seeks. Let him see you wear it and enjoy it."

"I don't know if I should do that," Natalie replied in a low voice.

"Yes, you should," Cheryl confirmed. "Trust me, Natalie. I know men. And I'm telling you, when a man sends you a gift like that, he's sending you a message. He likes you. Be gracious and keep the dress. Plus, Tanner can afford the dress. He'd be insulted if you give it back. Don't make that mistake."

Natalie's face lit up. "Okay, but you have to help me with my makeup and hair. I want to look as polished as you do. I only have an hour."

Cheryl didn't hesitate. "Let's get started, then. That's not much time for me to work my magic."

Cheryl and Natalie giggled and chatted through the transformation process. "One last thing," Cheryl said, and went to her tall jewel case to retrieve a necklace. It was a gold chain with a single pearl pendant. "Perfect," she said after putting it around Natalie's neck. "Take a look."

Natalie walked over to the full-length, three-panel mirror, stepping gingerly in her platform heels. She stopped at seeing her reflection. *Wow.* Even she had to admit she looked lovely. Natalie had never had anyone else do her makeup, but Cheryl was truly an artist. And her dark brown hair fell in large curls around her shoulders, down to her mid-back, and looked professionally styled.

"Thank you so much." She hugged her new friend. "He'll be here in a minute. At least I'll be presentable at this high-society fashion show."

"You're more than that," Cheryl confided. "You look ravishing."

14 – The Fashion Show

Natalie had never been to a New York fashion show, nor had she ever been chauffeured before. At home, if anyone did the chauffeuring, it was her. But all that paled in comparison to her excitement at being with Tanner. He got better looking every time she saw him.

He sat next to her at the show, in his soft beige jacket worn over a cream-colored shirt. The pants he wore must have been tailored to fit because they outlined his lean, muscled legs, hanging just so from his trim hips. His dark hair was thick and spiky. He looked so elegant and sexy.

He'd taken her hand to lead her inside, followed by two uniformed men that appeared to be part of his staff. He was greeted over and over, recognized by so many of the attendees. She saw the glances toward her. They all must have been wondering who the new girl was that he'd brought with him. Natalie breathed a "thank you" for the hundredth time for Cheryl's magic. At least she could attend without looking like a girl from rural America.

Tanner couldn't ignore the heat in his loins. He hadn't realized how difficult it would be to just sit beside her, especially with her wearing that dress. The black satin moved around her sensual curves, calling attention to them. Her dark brown hair gleamed as the lights played on it. Her innocence made her even sexier. The single pearl necklace she wore was unexplainably erotic. And she had a sweet aroma, all feminine and lavender. Oh, she was going to be his undoing.

The fashions were elegant. So many slinky, black designs were before her that Natalie was in a high-fashion daze. The models with makeup to accentuate the art of the design stepped by in their show-off-the-clothes walk. The show was on a wooden floor path, woven between the attendees, as opposed to a raised stage. It gave the buyers a closer view and friendlier experience.

The atmosphere was blasé, which

contrasted with Natalie's enthusiasm and wide-eyed admiration. She looked the part of the tourist and, at this point, she was. She had no intention of trying to fake it and pretend she'd been to hundreds of such shows. This was her first of many and she intended to enjoy it to the fullest. It didn't escape her notice that many buyers were taking notes. This was a business for them, not a holiday outing.

Natalie knew that one day the models would be showing off her designs and the buyers would be making notes about them. For now, she was dazzled by the wide variety of garments flowing by her. The electricity was infectious. Just seeing the creative designs on the confident, professional models gave Natalie goose bumps. This was where she wanted to be, in the high-fashion circles of New York and other fashion centers of the world.

Tanner's cock swelled with desire. He kept his eyes on Natalie, letting the fashion models flow by, unnoticed. His adorable dream girl, that he'd touched once so long ago, was beside him. He wanted her beyond all reason. She leaned forward to get a better view, and the swell of her breasts caused a flood of heat in his belly.

Her obvious excitement at attending her first show was irresistible. Her flushed cheeks and bright eyes reminded him all too well of the sweet orgasmic state he'd seen her so innocently experience that first night at the concert. He'd never forget it. That image had burned in his mind so many nights since then and he couldn't wait to get her alone.

15 – Lust

Tanner escorted Natalie out of the show the moment it ended, with the two men from his staff not far behind, not taking time to talk with anyone he knew. A cocktail party, by invitation only, was being held upstairs, and he wanted to go up. Natalie hesitated, knowing she'd be out of place. She wasn't used to the high-fashion crowd. But she'd be with Tanner, which gave her confidence.

He placed his hand firmly at her waist to guide her, possessively. Once upstairs, Tanner took two glasses of white wine from the waiter's tray and motioned to toast. "To your first New York fashion show," he offered, and tapped her glass, making a musical clink and taking a drink of the Chardonnay.

Natalie took a sip and it seemed to go straight to her head. She hadn't eaten much all day. She'd been too excited. And her adrenaline was still pumping from the show. It did taste good, though. She took another sip, watching Tanner smile and nod at various acquaintances that spotted him.

Tanner was a magnet for attention. He seemed used to it, and was very relaxed, giving his reserved smile at just the right time. Although many of them were buyers and people of importance in the industry, they looked like anyone you'd see at a cocktail party. Some women wore dresses and some were in pants. The men wore jackets but none looked formal; some were even downright casual. It gave Natalie the impression that they were all very comfortable in this setting. Only she felt nervous, knowing she was new to the scene and sure that it was obvious.

He took a small plate and loaded it with goodies, knowing Natalie must be starved. "Here, come with me," he commanded. He took her to another room, away from the other guests. The quiet was a relief. She hadn't realized how wired up she was. She took another sip of wine, wondering if she'd ever had more fun. She could think of only one time...

Tanner was behind her, his heat alerting

her to his closeness. He wrapped his arms around her and took her glass to set it on a nearby table. "I've missed you so much," he breathed into her hair, nuzzling her. Natalie felt a weakness flow through her and her sex tightened. Only *he* had this effect on her.

Natalie relaxed into his arms, leaning her head back against his chest. Her willingness fanned the flames of Tanner's desire. He grabbed her hair, pulling her head back to expose her bare neck. He kissed her cheek, under her jaw, and down her neck. She moaned softly, so enraptured to be with him once again.

Tanner bit lightly several times, up along her neck. His finger stroked along her jaw, sending sensual electricity through her. His hand cupped her face, turning her so she was looking into his lustful eyes. A split second of silence said all they needed to say to each other. His mouth pressed down, opening slightly, his tongue slipping in to rub and caress hers.

She caressed his tongue and pressed her body against his in open desire. If Tanner had any restraint left, it dissolved with her unspoken need. He reached behind her to unzip the satin dress and let it fall to her feet. Urgently, he undid her bra, freeing her lovely breasts. His hands held firm behind her back. He dipped his head down and sucked each hard nipple, repeatedly, until Natalie thought she would orgasm.

Tanner bit each nipple, causing slight pain, but Natalie marveled that the pain heightened her arousal. He looked at her red, swollen nipples and lifted her in one swift motion, carrying her several steps to a long sofa and placing her against the velvet cushions. Quickly, he undid his pants, stripping down to his boxer shorts faster than Natalie could fathom. The sight of his heavy, swollen cock was a vision of utter male glory. She took in her breath at the sight.

He dropped to his knees and spread her thighs with his strong hands, holding them apart so he could admire her succulent pussy. He groaned deeply with desire and leaned in to smell her sweetness and taste the cream in her moist cleft, eliciting a moan from Natalie. She arched her back and lifted her hips up, recalling the burning orgasm he'd given her so long ago.

Tanner reached for his pants, taking a condom from the pocket and ripping the package open. Natalie's eyes widened. She wanted Tanner and was desperate to please him. But at seeing him roll the condom over his hard cock, a surge of panic gripped her. He noticed the change in her expression and reached out to place his hand against her soft cheek. "What?" he asked softly. "Are you okay?"

Natalie looked away and Tanner didn't understand what was happening. His balls ached and his penis stood ready. The desire to plunge his huge dick deep into her innocent pussy was pulling him to take her. Yet even in his haze he knew that he would never take a woman against her will, and even more so, not an innocent like Natalie.

Tanner looked at her and froze. He'd answered his own question—an innocent like Natalie. It couldn't be that she was—*that innocent*. One more look at her face, turned aside in fear, told him he was right. He should have known. It was unlike him to be so imperceptive, so unaware. He'd let his blinding desire cloud his vision and that upset him. He'd have to regain control.

16 – Innocence

It was all so unexpected for Natalie. One minute she was burning with desire, craving Tanner's touch, and the next he was glaring at her, expecting more than she was prepared for. She felt guilty for not predicting it. She'd wanted him over and over in her dreams, but with his cock erect and ready to fuck her, she caved. "I want to go home," Natalie demanded, flushed.

"You'll be mine," Tanner threatened. His tone had shifted and a thread of intimidation laced his words. To her dismay, it only ignited her desire. She hadn't seen Tanner angry before. She wished she could be what he wanted, but she'd known all along she was inadequate. The miracle was that she'd had these special moments with him. She had no right to ask for more.

Tanner was aghast at the circumstances.

Normally, he could read women very well. He'd never had issues before. Not sure if he was right in his assessment of Natalie's reaction, he decided to back off. "I'll take you home," he said reluctantly, his eyes dark, his cock bulging with unrequited desire.

"No, I can get there on my own," she protested.

"I'm taking you," he commanded, and that was the end of the discussion. Both got dressed in strained silence. Tanner put his arm protectively around her shoulders to escort her out. She tensed at his touch but didn't push him away.

Safely in the back of the limo, Natalie risked a glance at Tanner to see if he was still angry. She wanted to look at him, thinking if she kept her eyes on him he wouldn't disappear. Yet she knew this would the last she'd see of him.

Tanner's face seemed to soften. He knew she was looking at him but he didn't want to face her. "I'm not used to someone like you," he admitted. His tone made it hard to resist him, such a gorgeous man.

He lifted her hand and kissed the top of it sweetly. He could be angry one minute and loving the next—so unpredictable. "Like what?" Natalie queried.

"So lovely and innocent," he said.

"I'm not innocent," she said, shaking her head, thinking of all the times she pleasured herself with visions of Tanner vividly in her mind and all her fantasies. If he only knew.

"Oh, really?" Tanner gave a subdued smirk.

"Yes, I've known lots of boys," she claimed, mustering as much boldness as she could.

"Yes, boys," he scoffed. "Well, now you're with a man—you've stepped into dangerous waters."

"Well, you asked me to attend this event" was all she could think of to say.

"How many men have you slept with?" he demanded, knowing he was overstepping his bounds, yet carried with the fury that boiled within him.

She was insulted. It was none of his business. Natalie's face was red, and it felt like her whole body was blushing from anger or embarrassment, she wasn't sure which. He was so exasperating. "It's none of your business!" she admonished him sharply, and turned to glare out the window.

Tanner dared not press. Even in his

blatant insensitivity, he knew when to hold back and wait for another time. He didn't understand her.

Women were not an issue for him. He had them when he needed them and they bent to his desires. Now he was faced with an incurable urge he couldn't satisfy, which infuriated him.

At Natalie's building, she leapt from the car as soon as it stopped and ran up the stairs without giving Tanner a chance to open the door for her. He fumed silently.

She needed to be away. She couldn't look at his beautiful, angry glare. She'd disappointed him.

Tanner watched her go inside to make sure she was safe before he directed his driver to take him home.

17 – Regret

Natalie burst in the front door, went straight to her room, and fell on the bed crying. At the moment, she was more angry than sad. She tended to cry when she got mad. She felt Cheryl sit down on the bed beside her. "What happened, honey?" she asked in a soft voice.

Natalie had no idea how she'd explain what she'd just been through with Tanner. "I'm a mess," she blurted out. "I'm so inadequate in so many ways. I don't know where to start."

Cheryl smiled gently. "Tell me what happened. Something must have happened."

Natalie rolled on her back and placed her arm over her eyes. "It was all going so well...the fashion show...everything. And then we went to the party. I was out of place, but as long as I was by Tanner's side everyone thought I was really somebody. But then it all came crashing down."

Cheryl stroked the length of Natalie's arm and lifted it away, uncovering her eyes.

"It's so embarrassing. I'm just not good enough for Tanner. He wanted..." And Natalie started crying again. Cheryl handed her a tissue, waiting patiently.

"We left the main room of the party and Tanner made a pass at me. Well, more than that. It was more than I was comfortable with. I rejected him. And now what will I do? He's become an obsession. He's all I want, but I'm not right for him."

"Well, now, I wouldn't jump to that conclusion," Cheryl reassured her.

"I'm not used to the big city. I'm out of my league here. But I can't go home. Fashion design is my career. I refuse to pass up the only opportunity I may have for design school. But if I stay, I'll run into Tanner again. Someone that prominent in the industry would be hard to avoid." Natalie dabbed her eyes, hoping her makeup wasn't smearing onto her dress.

"It's just all new to me, all of it. And he's so strong, so commanding. I never had a brother. I've never even had a father. How am I supposed to know how to deal with a domineering man? And that's what he is—domineering."

Cheryl laughed softly. "Yes, he is that. But that doesn't have to be the end. You just got off to a bad start. It's obvious you like him."

"Who wouldn't?" Natalie asked, not expecting any challenge to such an obvious truth. "He's perfect. I'll never want another man. And now I've ruined everything," she continued, revealing more than she'd intended.

Natalie was unable to relax. The idea of sleep was remote. Later in the evening, she called Jazzy, who was expecting to hear all about the fashion show. Natalie did her best to convey the excitement, but didn't have the heart to tell her about the incident with Tanner. It would only make Jazzy worry unnecessarily.

18 – Confession

Natalie washed off her makeup and changed into jeans and a T-shirt. It was still early but she didn't feel like doing anything, except moping. Her heart was crushed. After all this time, she finally met Tanner again and everything had blown up.

The truth was, his strength was reassuring to her. All her life, she'd had to be the strong one, taking care of her mother and her younger sister. There was no man around to count on, so she'd learned to rely on herself. A strong personality like Tanner's had never been a part of her life. She tended to reject what she wasn't familiar with. Yet, at the same time, Tanner's strength excited her.

The buzzer rang, indicating a visitor. Cheryl went, somewhat begrudgingly, to get Natalie. It was for her. Puzzled, Natalie went to the door and pressed the intercom. Cheryl didn't say who was downstairs, but she had a dark feeling that she knew. "Yes. Who is it?"

The baritone voice boomed through the speaker. "It's me, Tanner." Natalie fumed at his tone, although her heart raced at just hearing his voice. However, she was still angry at his earlier insult.

"What do you want?" she barked, not feeling nearly as angry as she tried to sound.

"Come downstairs, now," he ordered. Natalie expelled a frustrated sigh. If his idea of an apology was to order her about, he was misguided. She'd go down there and have this out with him.

Natalie grabbed her jacket and yelled a goodbye to Cheryl. "I'll be back later."

Catching sight of Tanner, standing alone in the lobby, wrenched her heart. There was something about this man that mesmerized her. She was drawn to him, clearly under his spell. There he was, dressed in casual pants and a light blue cashmere sweater. She felt slightly weak at the sight. He looked so debonair.

Without a word, he wrapped his arm around her and guided her out the door and into the back of his black limo. They were transported to a lovely hotel and he took her up a private elevator to the top of the building. She stepped through a door and onto the roof of the hotel, leaving the men who seemed to shadow Tanner everywhere standing in the elevator lobby.

The rooftop patio was decorated with outdoor furniture meant for entertaining. There was an iron railing around the edge of the roof and several sets of tables and chairs. The view was spectacular.

"I'm sorry, baby," Tanner said in a soft voice. "If I was too aggressive, I can go slower. I want you. I have to have you. Just tell me what you like."

Natalie looked at his Adonis face, his lustful eyes. She wanted him. Yes, she desperately wanted him. But what could she tell him? "I—ah, I don't know," she said regretfully.

"What do you mean you don't know?" he shouted before he could rein in his temper. "What kind of sex do you like? If you don't like it rough, I can slow down. Just tell me." He was calling her bluff, and he knew it, but ruthlessly continued.

Natalie's throat froze up. She wanted to tell him—something. But no words came out. She blushed crimson and looked down at her shoes, mortified.

Tanner looked at her, his earlier realization confirmed—her coyness, embarrassment and *the not knowing*. The look on his face softened. "You've never been with a man before, have you? Despite all your bold talk, earlier, about knowing boys. Knowing, yes...but never having sex. I'm right, aren't I?"

Natalie thought she'd die of embarrassment. She'd never felt ashamed before. But his hot look made her shrink back. Her silence was his answer.

"You're a virgin," he said definitively, as if it were a curse. He heaved a deep sigh and began to pace back and forth, pulling his hand through his hair. The confirmation of his suspicion annoyed him. He'd known she was a virgin when she'd looked away when he'd put on the condom. Yet, somehow, her admission infuriated him.

Natalie was distressed that she'd displeased him so much. That was the last thing she wanted to do. It had all been so romantic, so wonderful, and now this.

"But you went to college for four years," he said. "Nobody keeps their virginity through college," he restated incredulously.

At least not in his world, he thought sardonically. "You're a virgin," he said again, as if giving her another chance to refute him. "Come here, baby," he said sweetly.

She fell willingly into his arms, her anger instantly dissolved by his affection. She wanted to please him, wanted to love him and give him what he needed. But she knew she had failed so far. It never occurred to her that being a virgin would displease him. The whole subject never occurred to her, one way or the other.

Tanner hugged Natalie, holding her to his chest. His body relaxed and he accepted the situation. He'd have her, whatever it took. Letting her go was not a possibility. He'd not walk away from the challenge of possessing this innocent beauty.

He kept his arms wrapped around her, as if he didn't intend to let her go. And that was fine with her. Hope surged in her heart that he'd stay with her, just a little longer.

19 – Wanting

Natalie could have stayed in Tanner's embrace for the rest of her life. But he pulled back, holding her at arm's length, taking in her beauty. The flawless skin, big, dark eyes, and a sensual charm, which she exuded without being aware of it, sent a flood of desire to his loins. He stroked her cheek and rubbed his thumb along her lower lip. Pulling her back to him, he kissed her passionately. He was sweet now, not mad at her anymore.

She wasn't used to his changing moods. But she was relieved that everything seemed okay. Maybe there was a way. How he looked at her had a profound effect. Though he was still only twenty-six years old, his stern expression made him seem much more mature. He was commanding and, with his every look, made it known that he was in control.

Natalie hadn't had experience with letting anyone control her, especially not a man. But beyond the hard exterior, a man needing love—her love—clearly called to her. Was she imagining it? It didn't matter. Either way, she couldn't help but see his goodness and respond to it. The goodness he either wasn't aware of, or wouldn't admit to.

One minute he was angry, his eyes turning to blue glass. The next minute, he was hugging her sweetly. But he'd betrayed himself. No one could kiss her like he did and be heartless, as much as he'd have her believe so.

"What are you thinking?" he asked her, not able to read her face.

"I want you, Tanner," she confessed. Why was it that she told him the truth without hesitation? "I'm just uncertain what to do, I guess." That was the best she could come up with, and as soon as she'd said it, she wished she hadn't. He seemed to take this in, thinking it over.

He reached for her again, hugging her, feeling down her back and tugging her hair. He wanted to eat her up. He wanted every bit of her. It occurred to him that if he had any chance of protecting Natalie from his bad influence, he'd have to end this now. But then, he knew without question that it was already too late. He craved her and knew, as well as he knew anything at all, that he had to have her.

"I want you, too, baby. But not this way," he assured her. Natalie was lost. Was he saying he wanted her? How could she ever satisfy him?

Tanner sat on one of the patio chairs and lifted her onto his lap. She held her hands together looking down, unsure what he had in mind.

20 – Willing

Tanner gazed at the lovely beauty sitting on his lap. *She just has no idea how desirable she is. She's so humble—if only she knew.*

"I want you. But I want to do it right. The night I take your virginity will be a special night, a night you'll never forget." Natalie looked into his baby-blue eyes and felt the heat burn in her belly. *Yes,* she thought, *yes.*

"I'm taking you on a date first, a real date," he said, back in control. "I'll arrange everything. Are you willing?"

Willing, she mused. She was ready to do anything he asked, amazed he couldn't see that. "Yes, I am willing. Your wish is my command," she told him flirtatiously, and let out a small laugh, part relief and part joy.

"You may be sorry you said that," he replied, but there was a twinkle in his eyes.

"Before we go any further, there's something you need to agree to."

Natalie, already reeling from the date offer, didn't have a clue what else there could be. "What?" she inquired, looking at him as boldly as she dared.

"As you know, I'm a high-profile name in business. Not many know me personally. But publically, my sex life must remain confidential. I'm sure you can imagine what the press would do with intimate details about my bedroom habits.

"I'm often seen at events with women. They are primarily escorts; no one I'm personally involved with. For the most part, they are chosen for me," he told her.

Natalie attempted to get her wits around this conversation. She couldn't see why going on a date had become a publicity issue. If women were just escorts, that could mean he didn't date, or even that he was gay. All that didn't seem to fit with the man she was looking at. Those thoughts flew by in the second before Tanner continued his discourse.

"The women are very presentable, someone to be seen with. But there's never an indication of anything serious. A prominent bachelor, which I am, seen with a woman over any period of time, is a great story for the tabloids. I'm very careful to avoid that. I need your co-operation."

This was beginning to seem like a business negotiation, not an invitation for a date. "I think you are being paranoid," Natalie replied. "Any man can go on a date without it being a newsworthy incident."

"I'm not *any man*, Natalie," he said tersely. "And I'll need to know that you won't be talking to the press. My requirement is that, from this moment on, you keep our sexual involvement entirely private—from anyone. Understood?"

She couldn't imagine who she'd tell, anyway. The idea of talking to the press was so remote it was ridiculous. But she should be able to talk to her friends or family. Restricting that was absurd. "The only people I would ever discuss my relationships with would be close friends or family," she countered.

"Not even them," he said sternly. "No one—strict confidentiality is the rule."

"Maybe we should sign a contract and you can require that I'm bonded. That way you'll be properly recompensed if I misbehave," she said sardonically. "I can't feel that I have no one but you to talk to, when you're the one I'm sexually involved with. That won't work for me."

Tanner eased back a bit, knowing this wasn't a normal request. But then, he wasn't a normal man and his life was far from normal. "I know this seems odd to you," he said in a softer voice, "but it's very important to me. I can understand the need to have someone to talk with. You can talk to Cheryl, if you need to. I've known her a long time. I trust her."

Natalie looked into his blue eyes, allowing her gaze to include his perfect, handsome face. He seemed so sincere. This was really a concern for him. It wasn't like her to speak of relationships, even with close friends. All these years, she'd never told anyone of her sexual encounter with Tanner at the concert.

Really, she wasn't giving up much.

"Okay," she agreed. "Our sexual relationship will be completely private. I'm glad I won't have to be quiet with Cheryl. That would be uncomfortable, since I live with her. I'm not used to pretending with friends. But I'll comply with your wishes. It's unlikely I'd want to talk with anyone else, in any case."

"There's more." Tanner gave a little smile

but his eyes remained cold. A little shiver ran up Natalie's spine.

21 – Agreement

Tanner kissed the top of Natalie's head and ran his fingertips down her cheek, sending a thread of trepidation and sexual excitement, combined as one, through her body. He lifted her in his arms and sat her in the chair, directly opposite his.

Natalie prepared herself, not knowing what was to come. The look on his face was hard and unrevealing.

"I'm a dominant," he said without emotion.

Natalie thought of his domineering personality and wasn't surprised. But she hadn't heard of anyone called a dominant. "What does that mean, exactly?"

"It means I'd like you to submit to specific sexual activities that will be for our mutual pleasure. I prefer sexually submissive women. That doesn't mean I'll run your life. But in the bedroom, I'll have control." He looked at her, trying to judge her reaction.

"I've never been submissive. I've always had control in my life. I can't imagine giving that up to a man, no matter how desirable," she said with complete honesty.

"I'd like you to try it," he said without even flinching at her hesitation. "There's nothing to be afraid of. We'll set limits so we won't engage in any activity you're uncomfortable with, either physically or morally. You can have confidence that I will not do anything to hurt you. Nothing will leave marks or permanent damage. It's for my sexual pleasure, and even more so, for yours." Tanner reflected, with satisfaction, on all that he could teach her.

Natalie had no frame of reference. She'd never gone steady with someone, much less had sex. All this was a bit overwhelming. "Can I let you know?" she said timidly. "It's more than I'm able to conceive right now. I can't commit to such terms so early," she told him, wondering if that would end the relationship on the spot.

"Sure, baby," he said sweetly, reaching out to stroke her hair. "You are just so beautiful. I want you, in every way. I know this is all new. You've never had sex before. I want you to experience vanilla sex before we get into a more intense sexual experience. I just wanted to bring this up now, in case you wish to retract your earlier agreement to go on a date with me."

Natalie thought he looked more like a nervous young man asking her out than the billionaire control freak he really was. He always tried to come across as tough, but he couldn't fool her. She saw something in him, something kind and generous, and convinced herself of his goodness.

Her silence made him shift in his seat. He was at her mercy and he knew it.

She eyed him intently, fully aware, he'd gone from a position of strength to one of vulnerability in the blink of an eye. That vulnerability promised the intimacy she knew was possible, despite all his blustering and warning her away.

Now that she knew about his sexual preference, it was like he fully expected her to run away. Well, he didn't know her at all. "I'm not going to retract my agreement," she told him. "I want to go on that date with you, more than anything. If you're trying to scare me, it's not working." She laughed lightly.

Tanner was surprised at her calm, lighthearted manner. She disarmed him, never reacting as he predicted. He was relieved at her acceptance. "I'm so glad to hear you say that." He sighed, his eyes sparkling for the first time since the fashion show. Oh, how she loved it when his eyes sparkled.

22 – *Anticipation*

True to his word, Tanner arranged everything for their date. The first stop of the day was the Looking Glass Spa on the Upper East Side. The aroma of citrus and sandalwood wafted around her from the moment she entered. She was offered hand-blended tea and organic biscuits. Her package included more services than Natalie knew existed. She wished Jazzy were there to share with her.

She was very relaxed by the end of the sessions. She'd had the signature facial, the Swedish massage, and a complete waxing. Well, almost complete. She couldn't face a waxing of her pubic hair. She wondered if that was common with the women Tanner knew. He may be disappointed, but she wasn't ready to allow that just yet.

During the hours she was pampered, soft music played and drinks were replenished continuously so she wouldn't get dehydrated. Hydration is vital for vibrant beauty and health, she was told. Next was her hair and makeup. If she'd thought what Cheryl had done with her was impressive, it paled in comparison. Looking in the mirror afterwards, she hardly recognized herself.

Her dark brown hair gleamed with a shine she'd never been able to achieve before. It was piled up, with flowers positioned in a few key places. Select tendrils hung loose. Her skin looked flawless, if pale, but her cheeks had a blush of color that looked completely natural. Only she knew it wasn't. Her makeup was not overdone. It was just enough to make her look like one of the runway models, but a touch less dramatic.

Her skin was smooth and silky from the humidifying treatment. And her feet and hands were manicured and polished. She could really get used to service like this. It made her feel fantastic.

She'd balked at Tanner's itinerary for today, unwilling for him to break the bank for her. But he assured her that his company owned the spa and many of the other services she was to enjoy. He commanded her to submit to the day's activities, in preparation for a wonderful evening. She kept reminding herself that it would give him pleasure.

Her personal wardrobe wasn't even considered. A wardrobe consultant ushered her into a private dressing room and she spent an hour trying on different dresses. She selected a royal blue silk cocktail dress that was romantic, but not overly sexy. She'd have to edge into this at her own comfort level. The matching blue satin low heels were surprisingly easy to walk in.

No detail was left unattended. The consultant let her choose from a selection of fine French lingerie. She settled on a white lace set that was lovely and fit her slender curves just right. The outfit was completed with a small, delicately embroidered clutch and a light, yet warm, evening coat made of brown leather, a shade lighter than her eyes. It felt so soft around her that she was reluctant to remove it.

The final touch was the necklace chosen for the evening. It was white gold with brilliant-cut diamonds in the pendant. Natalie nearly fainted when she heard the price and hesitated to leave the room wearing it. Remembering Tanner would be with her all evening, along with several well-trained bodyguards, and learning it was insured against loss or theft, she was more relaxed. It was the loveliest necklace she'd ever worn.

Being prepped all afternoon helped take her mind off Tanner and the evening ahead. She drifted off for a few minutes during the massage. With the warm room, background sound of falling water, aroma of lavender, and the expert touch of the masseuse, she experienced the ultimate in relaxation.

But many times during the hair and makeup process when she wasn't chatting, she felt butterflies in her stomach. The combination of all this new luxury, and what she had to look forward to, had her alive and expectant.

She dreamed of Tanner, wondering how he'd be dressed and whether he'd be relaxed or stern. She wasn't used to him intimately. His mood seemed to vary and was unpredictable, although with what had been going on between them, it was understandable. All of it seemed like a wish come true and she prayed it wouldn't end, even though she knew it had to.

He was so gorgeous and perfect in every way. Ultimately, he'd find a woman up to those standards. Natalie didn't look as plain as she normally did. The beauty consultant, along with her expert team, had achieved the transformation they sought.

Tanner waited, watching the clock all day. He wanted Natalie with every fiber of his being and the prospect of having her kept him hard. He meant to possess her. That he could do this so completely was an added thrill. She'd be his and only his. He would make this night one she would remember forever. His inflated ego was further bolstered by knowing he would hold a place in her life that no other man ever could.

Dressing wasn't as involved for him as for Natalie. He'd been to many events, so his extensive wardrobe served him well. He chose an evening suit and gold cufflinks, understated but elegant. He had no desire to be flashy. The only person he cared to impress was his special date. He'd chosen to have a manicure and massage earlier in the day. He ran some gel through his thick dark hair and splashed on cologne.

In the back of the limo, on the way to the spa where Natalie would be enjoying a late afternoon drink of her choice, Tanner scanned his mental list to be sure he'd thought of everything. Satisfied, he leaned back, closing his eyes to envision the unfolding of the date he had meticulously planned.

He felt a pang inside and considered if what he intended was best for Natalie. Probably not, he admitted to himself. But he didn't have the will to alter the course he'd set, now that the woman he craved beyond all others was within reach.

23– The Date

Natalie had been on dates previously, but tonight was in a category by itself. Before she'd been chauffeured to the spa, a huge bouquet of flowers had been delivered to the penthouse. Cheryl had to clear off the table in the entry to make room for them, admitting she'd never seen such a large arrangement, and that was saying something. Cheryl had been sent many flowers, of all descriptions, in her years as a model and revered sex symbol.

Sitting in the overstuffed chair on the patio of the spa, Natalie glowed at the thought of the flowers. No one had ever given her flowers before, something every woman loved. It certainly set the tone for the special date. Now, sipping her handcrafted mint tea, she tried to relax—but it was impossible. He'd arrive in a few minutes. She was swept up in Tanner's plans for her and there was no turning back.

Without provocation, Natalie was thrown into panic when the old feeling of losing Tanner surged in her heart. What if he didn't show up for the date and she was left alone again—consumed with desire for him? She resorted to self-talk, telling herself it wouldn't make sense. There'd be no reason to arrange an all-day preparation for a date that wasn't going to happen.

Yet the nagging voice of her earlier disappointment wouldn't be muted until the attendant stood next to her and announced, "He's here for you." Natalie's heart raced and her legs felt a little wobbly. She took a deep breath and followed the uniformed clerk to the lobby. She was in for another surprise.

Tanner stood, elegantly dressed, in a lightweight suit with a shiny silver and black tie and a pale gray shirt with thin stripes. His hair looked styled, but oh so touchable. His gold cufflinks gleamed in the lobby light. His pale skin was smooth and perfect. He smiled his charming, boyish grin and Natalie grinned back.

"For you," he said, holding out a corsage of gardenias. She could smell it, even from a distance. He stepped forward. "I seem to recall that you didn't go to prom night. You ran off to a concert. And since I usurped that night, I don't want you to regret your loss. The least I can do is to provide a proper corsage and night out."

"Oh, Tanner, it's beautiful. You don't have to make up for that night. It was the most memorable night of my life," she said, honestly. She never seemed to hold back with him, against her usual instinct.

Tanner just smiled and wrapped the corsage around her slender wrist, lifting her hand to kiss her knuckles. "Shall we?" he said motioning to the door. Natalie felt a flush of excitement and nodded sweetly.

They had reservations at Daniel's, a romantic restaurant on the Upper East Side known for contemporary French cuisine. Tanner told her the chef had written several cookbooks and even had a TV show. For this special night, he was preparing a menu just for them, based on the preferences Tanner had submitted. When he'd asked Natalie a few detailed questions about her eating preferences, she'd never dreamed it would lead to such a special meal.

It was still early. Before dinner, Tanner had arranged for a carriage ride. Natalie couldn't imagine anything more romantic. Fortunately, the weather was warm enough for such a ride to be pleasurable. As the horses pulled the classic carriage through Central Park, Natalie looked around at the sights, just like the tourist she really was. Tanner admired her, pleased to see her enjoyment.

He placed his arm around her shoulders, pulling her close. She was glad to be wearing her leather coat. The cool breeze became chilly as the ride progressed. Natalie looked at Tanner, who seemed completely in his element. He was in charge and overtly seducing her. She couldn't believe her luck.

He was so beautiful, rich, and confident. What could she mean to him? Maybe he was using her, wanted her virginity, coveting the ego boost of being the first. Looking at him, sitting beside her, she was aware of his kindness, his generous nature that he worked so hard to hide. No matter what fate had in store, Natalie knew she wouldn't give up this date for anything. She'd cherish this night, no matter what happened in the future.

"You have bodyguards?" she asked, referring to the men she saw routinely, but only now realized the significance. Tanner shrugged as if it were normal to have your safety guarded.

"The consultant told me. I had been concerned about wearing this necklace in public." She laughed, slightly embarrassed at the opulence.

Tanner admired the delicate necklace and felt his heart warm at how perfect it looked around Natalie's slender neck. "Yes, it's wise to have guards. My father always did. I'm used to them. I'm not as well known by name as my father was. Yet it's easy enough to discover who I am. Do they bother you?"

"Oh, no—it's just different. I didn't even notice them at first. I guess they are trained to be unobtrusive. I hope they are enjoying the carriage ride behind us. It must be awfully romantic." Natalie giggled, recalling the two burly guards, who had stepped out of the dark vehicle that had parked behind the limo when they'd arrived at the park.

Tanner stroked Natalie's cheek with his fingertips. He'd been with many beautiful women, but there was something about her. Was it just that she was untouched by any other man? No, he didn't think that was it.

She had cast a spell over him, he thought

ruefully. He was trapped like a fly in a web. Her pale, creamy skin was flawless. And her long, brown curls, piled up on her head, were meant to be touched, pulled loose from the pins holding it so properly in place and allowed to flow free.

He wanted to bury his hands in her hair and nuzzle his face against her neck—her lovely, slender neck. He noticed her pulse throbbing gently at her throat. And her lips had an angelic quality, both innocent and seductive at the same time.

She was, quite simply, the most captivating woman he'd ever seen. Her unawareness of the effect she had on men made her all the more seductive. Her innocence and naïveté added a sumptuous, forbidden layer to his desire, already burning out of control.

"Tanner, do you ever think about the unlikelihood of our meeting? That night at the concert, I wouldn't have dreamed I'd run into anyone like you." She looked at him with admiration and longing she made no attempt to hide.

"Sometimes fortune smiles on us." He gave a stiff smile, but his eyes were serious. "When I was younger I would fly to venues just to see groups perform. My tastes run outside the norm. It seems yours do also.

"But that night, I just felt a desire to see that concert. I'm glad I followed my instinct," he said. "After that night, I didn't go back. I had many duties to attend to. I didn't have the freedom to just go whenever I wanted to, especially after my father passed away a couple of years ago. My responsibilities increased. I reap the rewards, so it's only fair."

Natalie's curiosity got the better of her and she asked what she'd been wondering for so long, "Why did you leave that night?"

Tanner shifted in his seat. He knew he needed to tell her, but had hoped to delay, at least until after this night. He didn't want to lose her, although he wouldn't blame her for leaving him. And maybe she should, before they passed the point of no return.

"You remember She Wants Revenge...the group that was playing at the concert?"

Natalie nodded. "Of course."

"Well," Tanner went on, "despite my better judgment, I really did intend to leave with you that night. There was nothing I wanted more. I'm sure if you were at that concert you had to be a fan and likely knew all the lyrics by heart."

Natalie nodded again to indicate he

should continue. She had no clue how song lyrics related to his disappearance.

"Yes, I'm not surprised," Tanner continued. "That group has a small but loyal following. Or they did have. I don't think they are performing anymore.

"Anyway, I was waiting for you in the lobby when you went in to let your friends know you'd be leaving with me. The group was playing one of their best songs called 'These Things.' I was singing along. And I had a premonition."

Tanner looked away for a moment, and then straight ahead, not really wanting to look at Natalie just yet. "I left before you returned, before we went any further. I'm bad for you, Natalie. I was then and I am now." Tanner looked at her loving gaze and felt a pain wrench in his chest.

"I don't see how you can say that," Natalie protested. "You've been very kind. I've enjoyed our time together. Well, most of it. I can't say I like being left without a word. But you're here now. We're together tonight. I'm here because I want to be—it's the only place I want to be. It's not like you forced me. I want to be with you. I want to be yours," Natalie confessed.

"There's something you don't know."

Tanner's face turned dark. "And I'm not prepared to tell everything right now. You're just so lovely and innocent. If you want me to leave you alone, just say so and I will. I'll take you home, directly."

"You're crazy," Natalie said, aghast.

"Yes, I might be, for taking you on a date with the intent to take your innocence, your virginity. You should save yourself for someone worthy of you," Tanner said seriously.

"You are worthy of me. Nothing can convince me otherwise. I am a good judge of people. You are kind and generous. I know that," Natalie pleaded.

"And you are naïve," Tanner cautioned. "I'm neither. I'm greedy, used to having what I want. And it's your fate that I want you, Natalie. I want you and I mean to have you. I suggest that when this carriage stops that you ask one of my guards to take you wherever you'd like to go, but away from me. And don't look back. If you do that, I promise I won't follow. I'll disappear from your life forever," Tanner stated.

Natalie was too surprised to respond. He sighed deeply, as if giving her warning was some kind of relief. "I warn you, I'm not good for you," he concluded.

Natalie didn't move for a minute. She wasn't sure how to convince Tanner that he was wrong. She knew it deep inside. Something had given him a false impression. He didn't know her at all if he thought she was that easily scared off.

She lifted her chin in defiance and said, "I consider I've been duly warned. Of exactly what, I'm not sure. But if you are trying to tell me you are a bad person, I'm not convinced. Either way, I'm not leaving. I want you, Tanner, as much as you want me—even more. So, unless you throw me out of this carriage, be prepared to see this date through as promised."

Tanner looked at her determined expression. She looked so vulnerable sitting there, so slender and defenseless. If he touched her, he'd take her right here in this carriage. He hesitated.

Her attempt at indignation pulled him into a lighter mood. He gave a tight smile and said, "Okay, since you think you are up to the task, let's go to dinner." Seeing his reluctant smile, Natalie smiled back, a brilliant smile of joy. This was going to be a special evening, she was sure of it.

24 – *Alone*

Dinner was quite a production. The chef started the meal with appetizers and champagne, and continued with gourmet treats paired with elegant wines. Dessert was cappuccino with tiramisu, Natalie's favorite dessert. Soft music, combined with the soft lighting and tasteful French décor, made Natalie feel like she'd been transported to Europe to have dinner in an authentic French restaurant. The white tablecloths, the candles, and the crystal chandeliers—all of it was so romantic.

Natalie was quick to show her pleasure, which warmed Tanner's heart. He was glad to share this evening with her. A small group played violin music on a stage in the corner of the room, just above a small dance floor. Tanner danced a slow dance with her, holding her close. Her heart was racing—

from his touch, his smell. And he could feel the warmth of her body pressed against him.

By the time dinner was over, Tanner couldn't wait any longer. He'd wanted Natalie from the first moment he'd seen her. Now, being this near, he felt urges that refused to be ignored. He guided her to the lobby and outside. The limo was waiting to take them to the hotel. Two security guards, ever at the ready, followed in the same dark vehicle that Natalie was used to seeing so didn't pay attention to, which was as it should be.

Alone in the back seat, with the privacy partition blocking the driver's view, he pulled her to him in one strong motion and slanted his mouth over hers, his need clear. A guttural sound came from deep within him at her soft, full lips, combined with the heady smell of her perfume and natural, feminine scent. His burning hot kiss was hard and possessive, letting her know his intentions.

Natalie slid her tongue inside his mouth. He'd already slipped his deep into her warm mouth and was caressing her tongue with quick, strong strokes. His desire inflamed hers, and she reached down, placing her hand over his hardness, bulging under his pants. Tanner moaned loudly and grabbed both of her hands, lifted them up, and pinned them against the seat.

"If you do that, baby, we'll never make it to the hotel," he groaned. "We're going to take this slow." He kissed her neck and bit her lower lip, tugging on it. "I've wanted you for so long."

Natalie felt her mounting arousal. Her nipples poked at the fabric covering them, begging for his touch. Molten heat flooded her lower body. She arched her back invitingly.

Tanner reached under her dress and rubbed his hand along her thigh, watching her cheeks flush. She rolled her head to one side in anticipation and Tanner leaned in and kissed her all over her neck and across the tops of her breasts, so tastefully exposed.

Thankfully, the ride was short. Tanner had known they'd never make it to his penthouse and had reserved a honeymoon suite nearby, at a hotel he frequented. He was checked in, keys in hand.

The hotel was traditionally designed and spoke of wealthy customers. Tanner and Natalie had eyes only for each other, not for the ornate décor floating past them. They stepped into an empty elevator and Tanner pressed her against the wall before the door even closed. He reached under the hem of her skirt to rub one hand over her firm buttocks. Natalie grabbed his hair in her fists, pulling him to her.

Needing no encouragement, Tanner kissed her with a passion that left her breathless, bruising her lips, and she wanted more. She kissed him back, licking, sucking, stroking his tongue and gently biting his lower lip with her teeth.

A single musical note signaled the elevator's arrival to their floor. Tanner lifted her in his arms and her head nuzzled into his neck, kissing and kissing. Neither one noticed or cared if there were any other guests in the foyer. They could have been in the middle of Madison Square Garden. They were aware only of each other and, at last, they could consummate their desire.

Tanner's cock pressed against Natalie and he feared he might come before he could get the door to the room open. He was struggling in his pocket for the keys while Natalie continued nuzzling and kissing and running her fingers through his thick, dark hair, oblivious to all else. The nondescript security guard stood in the shadows of the hall, where he'd been all evening, ensuring that Tanner and his date were safe and that no one else had been in the room.

At last, they were inside. Tanner slammed the door shut with his heel and strode purposefully to the bedroom, placing Natalie on her feet while he threw back the covers of the bed, but never removing his arm from around her waist. He'd planned to slowly undress her and extend the pleasure as long as possible. He could have her. She was to be his. The waiting was over.

25 – All Mine

Natalie sat, with glazed eyes, watching Tanner rip his clothes off. Such was her erotic state that she didn't seem able to speak and had no desire to alter the course of events. He was in charge and she placed her trust in him.

Tanner stood naked before Natalie, who was still fully clothed, not exactly sure what to do next. Her eyes were glued to his weighty penis, standing proudly before her. It was a stunning sight and her clit tightened instantly. She noticed he was fully waxed, no chest hair or pubic hair, and wondered if she should have had a full wax at the spa. Would he care?

He moved slowly toward her, and when he was so close she could feel his heat warming her, she leaned her head down and kissed his beautiful, hard cock. He moaned, low and deep, but stood still.

Natalie put her mouth over the top of his cock for a moment. She'd never done this before but had seen plenty of movies, so wasn't entirely clueless. His male sex smelled so good. She breathed in deeply and pressed her nose to his low abdomen, relishing the intimate moment. With one hand, she grasped the base of his hard member and placing her tongue along the shaft. She tasted up and down its length. She was lost in the unexpected pleasure.

"Enough," Tanner said, pulling her lovely face away and turning her chin up so he could look into her big eyes. "You are hot, baby."

He guided her to a standing position and kissed her deeply, tasting his own masculinity on her sensual lips. He proceeded to undress her, savoring the sight of her nakedness. The shoes, the dress, the corsage, the stockings, and garter were peeled away. He removed the delicate flowers from her hair and loosened it from the clips, to let it fall seductively around her shoulders.

Natalie stood frozen, her heart pounding. She'd never had a man undress her before. She didn't feel shy with Tanner. She always felt comfortable with him. She blushed anyway when he knelt to pull down her panties, never taking his eyes from hers. Before standing, he leaned in and kissed her dark, perfectly trimmed pubic hair.

Standing before her, Tanner reached behind and undid her lace bra, pulling it away from her creamy, firm breasts. He'd so often imagined what she would look like completely naked. He stepped back to take in her delicious body. She was more beautiful than he imagined. Her breasts were lush, her abdomen tight, her thighs slender. Her skin was flawless, pale and silky.

Her lips were sensual, with a slightly angelic quality, and her dark brown eyes held his gaze under a sweep of thick lashes. The only thing she still wore was the diamond necklace, which contrasted with her nakedness in a striking way. He reached behind her neck, found the clasp, and removed the ornament, placing it on the table beside the bed.

Tanner and Natalie stood, naked and wanting, for an instant in time, and then fell into each other's arms, kissing and feeling and touching. Tanner reached behind Natalie, running his hands down her back, grabbing her firm ass in both his hands and squeezing, sending new sensations through her.

Without warning, he picked her up and laid her down on the bed, kneeling over her. He lifted her arms over her head and grasped her wrists in one hand to immobilize her. His other hand played with her distended nipples, pinching and pulling. The pain caused Natalie's abdomen to tense in response, giving her a sense of pleasure over pain.

She rolled her head from side to side in an attempt to release the sexual tension building inside her. Tanner whispered, "Not yet, baby." He kissed her swollen nipples, as if to heal them. His kisses drifted down her sternum, her belly, and her inner thighs.

Tanner kissed and bit over her sex. Natalie whimpered. His tongue licked along her wet slit and he breathed in the smell of her arousal. His cock jerked in response. She was so sweet. He tasted the cream from between her inner lips. She spread her thighs, welcoming him.

His tongue swirled around her little pebble, tightened in preparation for orgasm. He used just the right pressure, enough to excite her, but not enough to allow her to come yet—not so soon. He released Natalie's wrists and used his other hand to open her outer lips. She felt the cool air flow across her sensitive tissue, a new sensation for her.

He put a finger inside her, gently preparing her. He moved his finger in and out. Natalie raised her hips and tensed her thighs. Tanner entered her again, this time with two fingers. Natalie was panting and started to beg. "Please, Tanner, please."

"Please what, baby?" he teased.

"Let me come. I'm going to come," she whined.

"No, not yet," he commanded. And Natalie emitted a tiny, tortured cry.

Tanner moved up Natalie's body, kissing and nibbling until he was beside her. She reached out and grabbed his hot, hard dick to squeeze it. He gasped and pushed his hips toward her, enjoying the immense pleasure of her sweet touch.

Her finger touched the hard knob of his penis, feeling the pre-cum. After dipping her finger in the liquid, she rubbed it around the bulging head and then squeezed him again. His groan told her she should continue. But Tanner was too close. He grabbed her wrist and said, "Stop or I won't be able to wait."

Tanner sat with his back against the padded headboard and pulled Natalie onto his lap so her butt was against his engorged cock, her back leaning against his chest. His hands cupped her breasts. His legs wrapped around hers and he pulled her thighs apart, exposing her vagina. His left hand continued to caress her breasts.

His right hand found her pubic mound and he placed his palm over the top. Holding her legs apart so she was unable to move away, he pressed down on her mound with the palm of his hand. Natalie felt a wave of pleasure. Tanner kept a steady pressure and began to make slow circles. The pressure radiated through her and her whole vagina flooded with sensation.

Her breathing sped and the muscles in her thighs tightened, yet her legs stayed wide apart. Tanner stopped the circular motions. Pressing slightly harder, he rubbed his palm up and down over her pubic mound, never releasing the tension.

Over and over, his palm moved toward her belly and then away, back and forth, back and forth. Natalie moaned loudly. The delicious motion pleasured her clit as if his hand were stroking it directly, and her whole body tensed in anticipation of complete release.

Tanner tortured her relentlessly with his palm. Her tight clit tensed in response to the stimulation. Natalie was in a pre-orgasmic state, eyes closed and head back, when Tanner's finger found the tip of her tiny clit. His finger flicked her most sensitive tissue in rhythm with the back-and-forth motion of his palm.

Natalie was consumed with want and heavy erotic waves started to engulf her. Her pussy tightened and pulsed. Yet Tanner continued the same motions, only faster.

Unable to move, and with violent orgasmic waves convulsing through her body, Natalie screamed—a long, high-pitched, breathy sound—pushing her head back against Tanner, who held her securely, holding and loving her until the last wave quieted and she relaxed in ecstasy.

Moments passed before Tanner moved his legs, freeing hers. He kissed her temple and moved aside to lay her head on the soft pillow.

"Tanner," she whispered. He looked so sexy, kneeling there beside her. His wide shoulders flowed down to his narrow waist and his heavy cock. Her eyes locked onto the amazing sight of him, a sculpture of perfection, smooth and muscled and ready for her.

"I'm going to make love to you, baby," he said sweetly. "You're mine." Natalie ran her tongue along her lower lip and reached out to caress his dick.

Tanner leaned over to retrieve a condom from the table next to the bed. An unknown feeling of excitement ran though her. She wanted to belong to Tanner. She wanted to give him all of herself, holding nothing back.

Tanner expertly rolled the condom over his swollen cock. He looked at Natalie's flushed cheeks, and it struck him how vulnerable she looked at that moment. She was so sexy and gorgeous, and she was his.

His hand touched her sex, feeling the wetness from her orgasm. She was ready. He watched her face as he spread her thighs and placed the knob of his cock inside her sweet pussy, holding his body over her, so as not to crush her with his weight. Natalie gasped.

"Okay?" he asked, and she nodded.

Tanner pushed more of his fat cock into her and his eyes closed as a wave of sensual pleasure flooded his abdomen and his cock pulsed. He pulled back a little, locking eyes with Natalie, seeing her glazed look and feeling his mounting arousal.

He pushed into her again, this time farther, and Natalie jerked but gave a slight smile of encouragement. The feel of her tight sheath around his aching member was wearing away his restraint. He pushed in farther and a little noise escaped from Natalie, letting him know he was close.

"It may hurt a little," he said, and then pushed all the way into her. She gasped and then moaned with pleasure. There was a quick, sharp pain, and then it felt so good. She'd never felt anything like it, having his huge cock fill her up. "I want you," she said, ignoring any temporary discomfort. The unbelievable pleasure was her only focus.

Tanner was an animal unleashed. He was inside her and her pussy gripped him tightly. He began to fuck her, slowly at first, and then faster. She spread her legs wider and grabbed Tanner's hair when he leaned down onto his elbows and kissed her. Tanner fucked faster and Natalie moved her hips to match his strokes, both of them panting heavily.

He raised his head and moaned, slowing his strokes to delay his release. Natalie's strong vaginal muscles tightened around his cock and her clit throbbed. She felt a familiar wave edge into her consciousness and knew she was on the verge of another orgasm. She'd never had one while being fucked, and it felt so good to feel the waves of passion begin to take her, with his hard cock filling her up.

"Yes, baby," Tanner whispered, feeling her start to pulse around his dick. "Come for me."

Natalie was already falling into another orgasm. She gave herself over to the power of it. She panted and moaned, driving Tanner out of his mind. His balls ached and his cock swelled; desire possessed him and he fucked without restraint. Natalie screamed quietly at the peak of her orgasm, sending Tanner over the edge.

"You're mine," he groaned and let go, completely. His orgasm held his body captive, running strong waves though him. His groin tightened and his penis pulsed repeatedly, shooting his thick cum inside Natalie in a heavy flow, giving Tanner the release he sought.

He came long and hard. Both Natalie and Tanner fucked slowly, long after the last wave of pleasure stopped. Finally, Tanner collapsed next to her with his arm around her, holding her against him. Natalie fell into a calm, dreamy state. She was his, really his.

26 – Pampering

Natalie fell asleep in a peaceful exhaustion. When she woke up, Tanner was not beside her. The light was on and she could hear the water running in the bathroom. She gave a relaxed sigh and stretched. The memory of sex with Tanner made her smile. Her body still glowed from the intense experience.

She looked at the bedside clock, noting that it was nearly eleven, and glanced up to see Tanner standing by the bathroom door. "Oh, you're awake," he said, his eyes soft. "I've run a bath for us."

He walked over to the bed, looking utterly delicious with just a towel wrapped around his waist, his hair still mussed and a satisfied look on his face.

He sat on the bed next to her. "How do you feel?" he asked.

"Wonderful." She smiled.

Tanner smiled back. "Well, you may be a little sore. Let's see how you are when you stand up," he said.

Natalie pulled back the sheet, exposing her soft, touchable breasts. Tanner felt his cock surge beneath the towel. He put his arms around her and gave her a long, sweet kiss, then guided her to the edge of the bed and stood, reaching back to take her hand. She stood on weak legs. The combination of the orgasms and the taking of her virginity had required stamina, and she was drained.

Tanner took her hand and led her to the bathroom. The huge sunken tub, which was the size of a small wading pool, was filled with fragrant bubbles. Her heart warmed. It was such a thoughtful thing to do. Tanner removed his towel and his hard cock caught her eye. She looked at him lustfully and he said, "Not yet, or at least not sex that way, until you have a chance to recover."

Natalie didn't feel like she needed to recover. She felt better than she'd ever felt and wanted more. Plus, she wasn't sure what he'd meant when he'd said "not sex that way." He must have another way in mind.

She thought back to their patio discussion about his sexual dominance. It interested her. He'd said it wouldn't hurt. Her first sex with Tanner hurt, but that was expected. The pain had been sharp and over quickly.

The bath was a Jacuzzi tub, and Tanner set the jets on a low speed. Natalie wrapped her long hair into a knot in the back to keep it from getting wet, and lowered herself into the warm water. It felt so good. "Ah-h-h-h," she said as she sank in the water. There were inflated pillows along the edge, so she leaned her head back onto one and closed her eyes for a moment. She noticed a minor burn in her vagina. The tissues were tender, but she was sure it wasn't a long-lasting issue. The bath should fix her. Tanner must have known that.

She opened her eyes to see Tanner looking at her. The water was up to his chest. He leaned back with his arms along the rim of the tub and seemed unable to take his eyes away from her. She felt embarrassed for a moment, realizing that she'd allowed him to fuck her, but the feeling evaporated. Looking at Tanner, she felt safe, comfortable—all his. And she was very happy.

"It feels good in here," she told him. "It's so relaxing. My muscles will turn soft if I stay under these massaging jets of water for long." She looked at him quietly for a moment and then revealed "Last night was wonderful for me." It felt so good, better than she'd expected. If she'd had any idea what she was missing, she may not have waited for Tanner, she thought smugly. On the other hand, he was very experienced and she wondered if she had given him even half the pleasure he'd given her. "Was I okay for you?" she asked.

Tanner smiled at the memory of sex with her. "Yes, baby. You were everything I imagined and more. And you are so beautiful. I don't know how I'll get enough of you," he admitted. "I want you again, but penetration is out. I want you to heal first. We have other options."

The smug look on his face made her curious. "Like what?" she asked.

"You'll see. But not now, just enjoy your bath," he ordered.

"Bossy, aren't you? Maybe I'd rather play," she countered.

Tanner's blue eyes locked onto hers. "Beware of tempting me," he warned.

Tanner reached for the soap and rag. He began washing her body, every delicious curve. His cock was hard under the water.

Once he was satisfied, he washed his own body and Natalie gasped when he stood. His cock was swollen and ready for her again. He enjoyed her lustful look, knowing her arousal.

"Not yet," he said, and guided her out of the tub, drying her with a soft towel. She felt like a treasured possession, the way he handled her. He made her feel different, special. She liked it.

"Let me dry you," she said, looking forward to touching his smooth, lean body. He smiled and handed her a towel. Natalie dried him head to toe, lovingly. All down his rock-hard form, she ran the towel, over his wide shoulders, his pumped biceps, and his muscled chest.

Then she got on her knees and dried down his ripped abdomen and down his legs, every inch of him beautiful. Last was his hard penis, seemingly ever ready for her. She put the towel around his waist, wrapping it behind him, and leaned her cheek against his hardness, hands on his buttocks, hugging him to her in a loving embrace.

Tanner stood still through the entire process, watching Natalie and enjoying her touching and handling of him. He placed his hands on the back of her head, holding her to him, feeling the heat rise in his loins. Delayed gratification was pleasurable, but the pain of waiting was surely torture.

Tanner lifted Natalie to her feet and leaned in to kiss her breasts, running his tongue over each nipple and noticing how hard they were already. He kissed up her neck, under her jaw, and found her warm lips. His mouth slanted over hers in a passionate kiss, and Natalie felt weak. She wanted him so much.

He found two plush robes and, after he wrapped them both, put his arm around Natalie's waist, taking her to the sitting room. "Room service should be ringing shortly. You must be hungry," he announced.

"You already ordered? How did you know I'd be hungry or what I'd want?" she challenged.

"Sex takes energy. I don't want you fading on me. And it's late in the evening. I thought scrambled eggs, caviar, and toast would be a good choice. And cappuccino, of course," he added.

She marveled at how he was always so controlled and had everything planned out. The date had been so organized and every detail attended to. Truly, it was the most romantic evening she could imagine. But she wondered if he ever did anything spontaneously. Anyway, she didn't mind him taking control this evening. She was sure it was only for this special night.

"Yes," she agreed. "Eggs do sound good. I am hungry. You do sap a girl's strength. But I wouldn't know about caviar. I've never had it. I don't see it on the menus back home." She grinned.

"Well, then, it's about time you tried it."

27 – The Truth

Tanner had delayed gratification as long as he was able. He knew the intimate touching and bathing had been a tease for them both. Through the late night meal, they nuzzled and kissed, wanting each other but waiting.

Once he felt Natalie was cared for, he took her back to bed. She noted the pile of sheets in the corner. It didn't escape her notice that he'd done a quick sheet change when she was in the bathroom. She'd seen some blood on the sheets, evidence of the taking of her virginity. After the bath and the food, she really felt fine.

Once he had her in bed, Tanner engaged in slow, intimate foreplay, arousing Natalie in a steady pace to a calming orgasm. And much to her surprise, instead of entering her he guided her hand onto his hot dick, showing her how to apply lubricant and rub him, just so. She was delighted that he enjoyed it so much, and it was a boost to her ego that she could give him release that way.

They fell asleep, satisfied and peaceful, in each other's arms. Natalie had never slept with a man before. Before drifting off, her last thought was that she didn't want to sleep alone, not anymore.

The next morning they awoke slowly, as lovers, not wanting to leave each other. Natalie felt warm and protected in Tanner's embrace. It was so right, so perfect.

"Good morning, baby," Tanner said.

"Good morning to you," she replied. "Last night was wonderful. Now I know what I've been missing all this time. But you were worth waiting for."

"It was special and wonderful for me, too," he agreed. His cock was hard for her already. He was insatiable where Natalie was concerned. He reached under the sheet and ran his hand over her soft, warm body.

Natalie purred, "Hmmm, more?" She turned on her side to stroke his early morning hardness.

"Yes, more," he groaned.

Natalie couldn't believe her fortune. She was so happy. It suddenly occurred to her that fortune had smiled on them, more than once. However unlikely it was that she'd met Tanner in the first place, the chance of their paths crossing a second time was even less likely. Yet they had. She puzzled about that for a moment. She'd never been that lucky in her life. It had to be Tanner.

"Where did you go?" Tanner said with a satisfied smile, caressing her cheek. "You seem to be far away."

"Oh, I was just thinking of us. How fortunate I am to have met you at the concert, even though all this time I thought I'd lost you. And then we ran into each other at the boutique," she said. "You just happened to be there, at just the right moment..."

She looked at Tanner's perfect face. Even sleep didn't mar his perfection. If anything, the sated look he had this morning made him even more desirable.

Something seemed to be rising to her consciousness, but she couldn't see it clearly. "With a dress that just happened to fit me perfectly," she finished.

Tanner's poker face didn't disguise his slight flush and he glanced away, removing his hand from her cheek like it burned his fingers. It was very uncharacteristic of him.

"What?" Natalie demanded, sitting up and pulling the sheet around her. "Tell me."

"Promise to hear me out. Don't be mad," he said.

"No promises until I hear what you are hiding," she teased. "Spill it."

Tanner ran his hand through his disheveled hair, hesitant to tell her. But he had no choice now. "I know you were upset the night I disappeared from the concert. The last thing I wanted to do was hurt you. I explained why I left, but..." He hesitated.

"Go on," she demanded.

"I wanted you from the first moment I saw you. I won't deny that. I left with the best intentions of leaving you alone and letting you get on with your life. But even before I was back to my hotel, I knew I couldn't let go. I guess I didn't want to. I didn't see the harm in finding out more about you. As long as I didn't interfere, what could it hurt?" He seemed lost in thought.

Natalie propped herself up on her elbow, her eyes intent on him. "Go on," she requested.

Tanner took a breath, mustering his courage. If he lost her now, he didn't want to think of how that would feel. But she knew something was up.

"I had asked your name before we parted. It was easy enough to find out where you lived and find out more about you. There are not that many Natalie Bakers in Oakland that were graduating high school that year.

"I discovered through my private investigators that you led a quiet life. You worked as a seamstress with your mother. You didn't seem to go out much that I could tell. You attended your local college, so you could stay close to home, I guessed.

"When I learned of your application to the design institute, it got my attention. I know you've been designing clothes since you were a little girl. So I wanted to help. I probably shouldn't have interfered, but it's too late for recriminations."

He looked at Natalie's surprised face. The pieces were beginning to fit together. "You know an awful lot about me. You were watching me? You had me followed?" Her face wasn't accusatory, more surprised. Tanner just looked at her, his face blank.

"And the scholarship to the institute, you must have helped with that. It was unlikely that I'd be chosen," Natalie stated. Another thought occurred to her. "And meeting you at the boutique—it wasn't by chance, was it? You knew I'd be there then." Instantly, all became clear. Yes, Natalie had never seen such good fortune before her encounter with Tanner.

"And you just happened to have a dress that fit me perfectly that you wanted me to model," she said, beginning to feel rather manipulated. "The casual invitation to lunch, the fashion show...it was all under your perfect control."

Natalie took a moment to get her wits around what had happened. "You should have told me," she said, miffed. "It's my life. I don't appreciate being watched and controlled. Destiny is one thing, but this is going too far. I've always made my own way. I don't need you seeing that I get unearned scholarships, or..."

Another distressing thought sprang to view. "Cheryl. She was so generous to let me share her penthouse. It's so elegant. Surely any accommodations I'd have secured wouldn't be of that scale. You know her and trust her, you said. I never had to give you her address. You knew where she lived and had been there before. You asked her to offer me a room. It wasn't her idea, was it?"

Natalie sagged at the realization that she

was imposing on Cheryl, who'd only offered her lodging at Tanner's request. And if she knew anything, she knew that Tanner was not easily refused.

Tanner made an attempt to placate her. "Cheryl does prefer company. She likes you. I didn't force her to let you stay there. It was just a suggestion."

"And that's how you knew I'd be at the boutique that morning. Cheryl called you when I left. She'd suggested I stop by there—at your direction no doubt." Natalie's irritation was rising. She'd been independent her whole life. There'd been no one to care for her, and certainly no one controlling the path her life would take. It was all too much.

"Are you mad?" Tanner asked flatly.

"Yes, I'm mad," Natalie retorted. "How would you feel? Oh, well, don't answer that. You have taken liberties with me. And I don't just mean taking my virginity last night. You have influenced my life without my consent.

"I should be grateful, I suppose, because of the benefits. But it's hardly deserved." Tears rolled down her cheeks, increasing her frustration at crying once again when she was angry, which she always seemed to.

Natalie stood on shaky legs, grabbing a blanket and wrapping it around her, embarrassed to be naked in front of Tanner right now. She felt so violated.

"Where are you going?" Tanner asked, fearing the response.

"I'm leaving," she declared.

"Shall I call you later?" Tanner asked, keeping his composure.

Natalie fumed. "I'll let you know." And with that she grabbed her storybook satin dress and undergarments and stalked into the bathroom to get dressed.

28 – Apart

Natalie felt an emptiness inside her that ached, never abating, only worsening. True, she was mad at Tanner. She couldn't abide dishonesty, no matter how well intended. She hadn't seen him in two days. At least he'd respected her decision. She told him she'd let him know if he could call, and now, she desperately wished he would do just that.

The flowers he'd sent her before their date no longer graced the foyer. She'd thrown them out, because she couldn't bear to look at them, such was her pain. She was in unfamiliar waters and didn't know what the right course of action was. She was already in over her head.

Her brief call to Jazzy that day was difficult. She tried to sound cheerful, telling her about the spa, the carriage ride, and the dinner. But Jazzy knew her too well and sensed something wasn't right. Natalie assured her that everything was fine. Everything was just all new and overwhelming.

But Tanner had become an obsession and she continued to want him, despite any misgivings. She'd never given herself to another man. It had never been an option. No one else stirred desire in her the way he did.

Thinking it over, she could even understand why he did what he did. If she had known his full name and where he lived, after their first meeting, what might she have done? Could she really blame him?

He was a man of wealth and power, used to commanding and controlling. He was doing what was natural for him. He'd clashed with Natalie's innate sense of what was right. Still, the truth was she didn't want him any less. He was the man she wanted, and she'd have to face that. Whatever that entailed was to be her fate—speaking of destiny.

Tanner left Natalie alone, as she requested. He'd given her the chance to occlude him from her life, more than once, but she hadn't taken it. Now he'd taken her for his own and found he craved her beyond endurance. Only by losing himself in work, was he able to keep from calling her.

He dominated those around him. He knew that about himself. It appeared that didn't sit well with Natalie. She was not only innocent, but independent of spirit. Tanner hadn't encountered that before. Women were willing to be cared for and protected. He'd thought that was the right way, but Natalie had a different view of matters.

Tanner could take or leave any woman, he'd told himself. Then how was he to explain his unrelenting desire for one slender, seductive woman? He meant to have her completely. For now, she needed time, but he had every intention of keeping her. He had the desire and he had the power. He only wanted the best for her. She'd have to get used to the fact that he could provide it. And he would.

Cheryl knocked on Natalie's bedroom door. "Natalie?" The door opened. Natalie didn't say anything. The sad look on her face said it all. She just went back and sat on the bed, pulling her knees up to her chest.

Cheryl sat next to her and looked at her long and hard. "Natalie, are you okay, honey?"

Natalie shook her head, burying her face in her hands, softly sobbing.

"Can you tell me about it?" Cheryl asked in a kind voice.

Natalie hesitated a moment to get her thoughts together. She so desperately needed to confide in someone. Jazzy would care but she didn't want to burden her. She was at home, taking care of mother. The last thing she needed to hear was that Natalie was crushed after less than a week in New York. And now with the confidentiality, it would violate her agreement if she were to tell her sister. It all felt so confining and out of her control.

"I'm in trouble," she started, and poured out her heart to her attentive friend, starting with the unforgettable encounter at the concert and through all the events leading up to her untenable situation. When Natalie shared her most private thoughts and informed Cheryl that she was no longer a virgin, the magnitude of the upset was clear.

"Listen, honey," Cheryl said. "First of all, you are welcome here. Tanner does not give me orders. I was pleased at his suggestion of inviting you to stay with me. Please, don't give that another thought.

"Now, on the subject of Tanner...oh, where to begin? I know you don't have a lot of experience with men and I willingly admit I'm not an expert. I've had my share of dramatic breakups. But I do know that Tanner is a good man. With all that business about him being bad for you, it seems he's trying to protect you.

"But I know that if you let this relationship pass you by, you'll always regret it. You've had Tanner in your heart since the concert, over four years ago now. Do you really think you can just walk away?" Cheryl asked.

Natalie's heart swelled at the thought of her feelings for Tanner. "No, I can't walk away. Maybe I should, but I won't be able to. I want to be with him, whether that's the right decision or not. But how can it be wrong to be with someone you love? And I know I love him. He doesn't know that, but I've never been more certain of anything." Just voicing her feelings made Natalie feel better.

"Well, let's do something about those red, swollen eyes. I have a few makeup tricks that might help. And you call Tanner to patch things up. I'm sure he's in just as much pain as you are."

29 – Starting Over

Tanner had agreed to meet Natalie at a nearby coffee shop. She looked as sexy in her beige slacks and wool blazer as she did in the satin dress. Tanner had missed her. He couldn't take his eyes off her.

"I know you don't want me to mess with your future without consulting you. I'm glad it's out in the open now. From now on, you'll know of any plans that concern you," Tanner assured her. "Are we okay?" Although Natalie had done her best to disguise it, he could tell she'd been crying recently.

"Yes, we're okay." Natalie gave a weak smile. Possibly her heart would mend if she sat here looking at Tanner long enough. She never wanted to be separated from him again. "I just want us to be open with each other."

"I'll do my best," he said. "I'm used to being in control. My business depends on it. In my private life, it's been the same. I was just looking out for you. From now on, I'll make an effort to get your consent.

"And just so you know, that scholarship was deserved. I've seen your work. No one lost out. The yearly scholarship was given out as it always is. I created a new one for you and future students will benefit from it, now that it's been set up."

He was incorrigible, but so impossibly handsome. "I can't believe you created a new scholarship for me. Thank you," Natalie said graciously. There was no point in arguing about it now. It was done. "When I'm a successful designer, I can pay it back." He may have control, but she wasn't ready to give up her pride by taking handouts.

Tanner found her frustrating. He couldn't fathom why she objected so harshly to him seeing to her welfare. "You're not paying it back," he said with authority. "There's no need to."

"Okay then, I'll help some other struggling designer afford to go to the institute," she said stubbornly, holding her ground.

"If you keep that up, I'm going to grab

you, right here in this coffee shop, and spank your bottom," Tanner whispered intimately, leaning in eye to eye.

Natalie couldn't believe his arrogance. At the same time, with his face only inches from hers, the idea of him spanking her bare bottom was exciting. It was a new excitement for her. She should be offended at him thinking he could order her about. Yet she felt a familiar heat in her lower body, betraying her overpowering need for him.

Tanner looked at her boldly and her cheeks colored. "Let's get out of here," he directed, taking her by the hand and leading her to the front of the shop, where the limo waited.

30 – Experimentation

Tanner's garden penthouse, on the Upper East Side, was like a mansion. Natalie's eyes widened, trying to take in the panorama. It was so different from her home that she felt it was more of a royal palace than a home. The view from the outdoor patio was unbelievable. The New York skyline was in plain view, almost as if she could reach out and touch the high rises.

The long main room was lushly decorated in gold and brown tones, with carpet so thickly padded that Natalie felt springy when she walked on it. Tanner led her into his drawing room, with wraparound windows and almost aerial views of Central Park and the Metropolitan Museum of Art. Along the patio rim, she could see terraces with box hedges and huge planters blooming with river birch trees.

There were climbing roses, which looked almost surreal, reaching up to the sky against the outline of Manhattan.

In the bedroom, the floor was covered in the squishiest, woven sage-green and cream carpeting. The huge bed was the centerpiece, with masculine dark wood for the headboard and a canopy tied at the four corners with sheer fabric. A long, overstuffed ottoman was positioned at the foot of the bed. The heavy emerald-green velvet drapes were open, allowing bright light to illuminate the sensual room. Under the window was an emerald-green trunk. She wondered what Tanner kept in there.

"This is quite a place," she said. "This is where you live?"

"When I'm in New York," he told her. She looked at him, remembering his threat in the coffee shop to spank her. Her cheeks flushed. Would he really do that in public? The picture of him doing that should have distressed her. Instead, she felt excitement consuming her.

The bedroom was quiet. Tanner looked at Natalie, who stood very still. Their desire was not to be ignored. "You've made me angry," he said, catching her off guard. "I want to spank you."

Natalie's cheeks turned pink. She thought of several smart replies, but no words came out. Why was she so turned on? With her eyes focused on the thick carpet, she finally mumbled, "Why?"

"I want to do things to make life better for you. You rebelled. Worse yet, you left me, for two long days. You deserve a spanking." Natalie continued to study the carpet, unable to look at him. His admonishment didn't offend her. Instead, dark desire rose within her, a desire only he seemed to stir.

Tanner stepped closer to her and, lowering his voice, he continued. "I told you I like...to dominate. The idea of having your bare ass over my lap, and spanking it until it's red, turns me on. It will hurt you, and I get pleasure in that. But I think you'll find pleasure, more pleasure than you imagine right now. You told me you'd consider trying things with me. Have you considered?" He touched her cheek and lifted her chin to look into her eyes.

She saw a stern expression she wasn't used to. *This is Tanner*, she told herself. *He won't hurt me.*

"Well?" His eyes turned dark.

Natalie's thoughts were confused. She

wanted Tanner and, for some reason, the idea of him spanking her was very erotic. She wanted to please him, and he wanted to do this. He had a shadow of violence in him that had sparked her sexually, since the first time he'd touched her, so long ago. She couldn't explain it, nor could she deny it.

She gave a slight nod of her head, indicating her agreement. The gleam in his eyes both scared and excited her.

"We'll do it easy this first time. Come here," he said, and pulled her to the bed. He sat down and looked at her. She was unable to read any emotion in his face. "Pull down your pants," he commanded in an even tone. Natalie's heart pounded.

Not believing she was doing this, she unbuttoned her pants and pulled them down to mid-thigh. "All the way," Tanner ordered gruffly.

Natalie reached for the waistband of her pants, and leaning over, pulled them all the way to her ankles. "Now your panties," he directed. A stab of anxiety ran through her, but she willed her hands to grab her silk panties. Cautiously, she pulled them down—taking way too long, she was sure—all the way to her ankles.

She looked with trepidation into

Do you love Emily Jane Trent's romantic tales?

Let her know by telling her what you liked in a review, and leaving stars! It helps other readers make good buying decisions – they listen to you.

Tanner's eyes, trying to find the gentleness of the other night, but there was none. "I warned you to go away, didn't I?" She nodded at him in affirmation.

"You stayed. Now you'll pay for it," he barked. She hadn't anticipated his next move. He grabbed both her wrists and pulled her to him and over his knee. She felt the cold air on her bare butt. Fear did not overtake her. In its place was a flood of heat to her vagina, causing her clit to tighten, and he hadn't even touched her yet.

She braced for the blow, but it didn't come. Instead, she felt his warm hand on her ass cheeks. He rubbed his hand over them with admiring touches. "Your tight little ass is so beautiful," he said. "I'm going to spank you and make your bottom bright red. You've angered me. Do you understand?"

"Yes," Natalie answered weakly.

"Six strokes," he warned. "One," he said, and the palm of his hand hit her bare butt on the soft, fleshy part, making a loud smacking sound. Natalie yelped. "Be quiet," he ordered. "Or the spanking will be worse." Before he continued, he gently rubbed the spot where he'd just spanked her, as if to heal the pain.

"Two," he called, and the smack of his hand stung her bare skin. She felt tears in her eyes, more from the shock of the experience than pain. It stung but didn't hurt, not really.

Tanner continued counting, and between each spank he'd caress her stinging skin. "Six," he said with finality. And Natalie was so turned on she thought she might come, just with him caressing her red skin. At the same time, she was upset with herself. She knew this sort of thing was only done privately and she shouldn't be enjoying it. Yet she *was* enjoying it—she thought she was, anyway.

She felt duly chastised and somewhat humiliated, but she'd given Tanner what he needed, and that pleased her. "Okay, baby. That's over," he told her, rubbing her bottom. "Stay on my lap," he said kindly, seeming to change mood. He reached into the nightstand drawer to find a small tube. "I'm going to put some of this on you. It will help with the sting." Tanner rubbed some cool gel on her sensitive skin.

He eased her off his lap so she was stretched out on her side next to him, and he pulled part of the comforter over her to keep her warm. Her butt stung, but not a lot. "Don't make me angry again, baby," he whispered.

Natalie covered her face with her arm to hide the tears that refused to stop. A rush of different emotions swamped her.

Tanner took a tissue from the nightstand and handed it to her. "Are you okay? Did it hurt too much?" he asked sincerely.

Natalie was relieved to have the kind, gentle Tanner back. She was puzzled by his mood shifts. "No it didn't hurt, not really. I'm just confused." She sobbed quietly.

"Did it feel good? Tell me, how was it for you?" he asked.

"I...um...I don't know. I'm turned on, but you were punishing me. No one has ever done that. I must have a dark side, dark desire that I've never discovered before. I shouldn't enjoy it, should I?"

Tanner lifted her arm away from her face and cupped her chin, so she was forced to look at him. "What we do together is for our pleasure. I'll never do anything you don't want me to. But if you are willing, pain can push you to your limits of pleasure. Do you think you'd let me do that again? Would you experiment with me and see what else you like?"

Natalie couldn't believe she was agreeing,

but she nodded her head. Being with Tanner was special. He could be so sweet and so romantic. She didn't understand why he needed to punish her and what caused him to be so stern. But she trusted him, for a reason she couldn't state. And she wanted to have sex with him, again and again.

"I want to give you pleasure," she confessed. "I'll try. I can experiment. But don't be too rough with me, okay?"

"I won't, baby. I'll never push you past your limit. We're going to talk about that. It's best if we understand each other's desires, and also each other's limits," he explained.

Natalie's sex clenched and her clit hardened. She could still feel the sting of the spanking on her bottom, which increased her arousal. "Will you make love to me?" she said to Tanner, unable to hold back her honest desire. She sensed that a door had been opened, a door to pleasure she'd never dreamed of, and that door could not be closed again. This gorgeous, sexy man was hers and she wanted him, more than ever.

31 – Sweet Reward

Tanner's lovemaking was sweet, even sweeter than the first time, if that were possible.

He lifted her in his arms to turn back the covers then sat with her on his lap. Her red ass was still tender, but not much. He'd been easy with her, spanking her the first time. Tanner kissed her tenderly, losing his hands in her thick hair, plunging his tongue deep into her mouth. His deep groan gave her pleasure.

Natalie could feel his erection growing under the cloth of his pants, pressing against her nakedness. He stood, placing her on her feet so he could rapidly undress. She'd seen him naked before, but the perfection of his muscled form still took her breath away.

His cotton briefs came off in one fluid movement, allowing his hard dick to spring into view. Her hand wrapped around his hot member and she squeezed, enjoying the feel of it. Tanner's eyes briefly closed.

He picked her up and got in position on the bed with her on top. She held her balance by placing her hands on his shoulders. They felt like rock under her soft palms. Even that served to excite her, hardening her nipples.

Tanner gazed at the beauty above him. Her skin was pale and silky smooth, revealing no imperfections. Her dark, chocolate-brown eyes were glazed with sexual arousal. Her glossy brown curls fell forward, touching the tops of her firm breasts. Her taut belly was tensed in anticipation.

Her mouth was so expressive. It was sensual, yet innocent at the same time, and so kissable, so desirable. Natalie had an endearing quality of innocence combined with sexuality—an explosive combination for Tanner.

He reached up to flick her red, protruding nipples, and Natalie whimpered in response. He cupped each soft breast in his hands, owning, possessing. *She's mine—all mine.*

Natalie had never had another man. This

added to her allure. Tanner hadn't purposely sought out a virgin. But having found one, the idea that he—and only he—possessed her sent desire coursing through his body. The lust she stirred within him was beyond endurance.

Without warning, he put two fingers inside her, causing her to gasp. A new heat flooded her loins and her clit tightened. She tossed her head back, her long hair flowing down her bare back and touching Tanner's lean thighs.

"Tanner, Tanner," she purred.

His thumb found her little pearl, just inside her labia, at that most sensitive spot. He caressed her, relishing in her moans and pleadings, yet removing his hand just before she went too far. She began to beg. "Please, please," she moaned.

"What, baby?" he whispered, excited by the erotic torture created by delay. He reached to the table beside the bed and deftly grabbed a condom, unwrapping it, lifting Natalie, and swiftly rolling it over his huge cock. She never stirred from her aroused state.

"You're so wet," he commented with obvious pleasure. "You're hot, aren't you, baby?"

"Yes, yes, Tanner. I need you," she gasped.

She felt the tip of his penis touch her vagina and cried out, the excitement escaping her lips without prompting. "Ah, ah," she panted.

Tanner held her hips in both his hands, controlling her movements. He lifted her away from his hard cock. "No," she protested.

"Tell me what you want, baby," he choked out. "I need to hear it."

"I want you inside me, please. Inside me, please," she said throatily.

Tanner plunged his cock into her halfway down and she gasped with the suddenness. Her panting grew louder and faster. He pulled back again, as if to tease. But his need was great and he could not stay back.

This time he plunged into her, all the way. He heard her high-pitched scream, short and breathy, causing him to come close to losing control. Tanner moved inside her, slowly at first. Natalie tried to move up and down on his hard rod but he held her tight, not allowing her to over-stimulate him.

Natalie began to fall into a state of sexual tension bordering on pain, craving satisfaction. The cool air of the room touched her body and her bare ass stung from the earlier spanking, but just enough to remind her. Her clit hardened, her nipples ached. Single-minded, she wanted only one thing: to rub Tanner's delicious cock inside her and propel herself into a powerful orgasm.

But he wouldn't allow it. Each time she neared orgasm, he knew and stopped moving. The agony was total. He seemed to know how far he could take her. Just when she was sure she'd lose her mind, he began to move faster and, not stopping, fucked her with violence.

She helped him, pushing up and down on him, relentless and wanting. Tanner panted heavily and pushed his hips up and down to assist her efforts. Together they rode into an all-consuming orgasm. Nothing existed but each other, and the throes of orgasmic waves that took them both over the crest. She screamed loudly and with abandon.

Fucking hard, fast, and relentless, Tanner still managed to hold back until he felt the strong muscles of Natalie's vagina convulse around him. He let go and plunged into his orgasm, simultaneous with hers. Tanner moaned deeply, and willingly relinquished control to the powerful erotic waves.

Glowing and warm all over, Natalie's slender form relaxed and she collapsed on top of Tanner, her head nuzzled against his neck. He was unable to move for several seconds.

It's a dream, a wonderful dream, Natalie thought. She hoped she never awoke. After a few moments, she felt Tanner's hand gently stroking her back. Up and back down, then over her tender buttocks. She sighed in contentment.

32 – Commitment

Natalie fell asleep with Tanner holding her. When she awoke, she was alone and unsure for how long she'd dozed. For a moment, she didn't remember where she was, but the warm, loving feeling inside her was all she needed to recall being in Tanner's arms not long before.

She found a robe in his closet and wrapped it around her. Tanner was in the huge kitchen, preparing food. "You must be hungry," he said. "I've made an omelet." His grin made a unique brand of happiness radiate through Natalie.

"You cook?" she inquired.

"Yes, a bit," he told her. "I gave my cook the day off. I can manage. Eggs...not such a big challenge." His deep, male laugh of pleasure showed a lighter side of him. He did have a sense of humor, Natalie was sure.

Out on the patio, they ate their omelet, toast, and coffee. Even the compelling view couldn't pull Natalie's attention away from Tanner. He was a puzzle to her. Admittedly, he got pleasure from punishing her and, shocking though it had been at the time, she enjoyed it.

Yet he could be so sweet. She wanted to make love with him, endlessly. Why had he waited so long?

She looked at him intently, pulling his attention to her. "Tanner, why did you wait? We could have been together four years ago. I had no idea where to find you, or I would have tried. Yet you were keeping track of me the whole time. Why didn't you ever call or come to see me?"

Tanner's baby-blue eyes turned dark, as did his mood. "I'm not good for you," he said flatly.

"How can you say that?" she gasped. "These have been the best days of my life."

Tanner looked at her, unable to understand her. She confused him. She'd been a virgin such a short time ago. Yet she satisfied him, as it seemed no other woman could. He wanted her and intended to keep her as his own.

"It's not a healthy relationship. You should date someone that is able to be intimate with you in ways that I cannot. I tried to stay away. As long as you were in a different city, I could hold back. But if I don't have to get on a plane to see you, if you're so close like you are now... Well, I won't be able to resist. I should, but I won't. I'm a greedy, self-centered man.

"I want you, Natalie. I want you completely. I intend to do things with you, things you have no idea of right now. I will give you sexual pleasure and take my own. I have strong needs. As long as you are willing, I'll see to your needs and give you experiences you've never dreamed of. But that's all I can give you. Do you understand that?"

Natalie looked into his eyes, so dark now. She heard what he said, but it didn't seem to match what she knew of him. His kindness and ability to give her pleasure went way beyond what he would have her believe. Looking into his cold eyes, it was clear to her that now was not the time to try to change his mind, to try to show him what he really had to offer. She knew the truth, yet it was a reality he had yet to grasp.

She knew one thing beyond any doubt.

Tanner was the man for her, and no other. His attempts to scare her away were pointless. She knew she wasn't going anywhere. It wasn't that she was especially brave. It was just that she just wanted him, beyond all reason. He did something to her that she knew no other man ever would.

Her prolonged silence had Tanner worried. He shifted in his seat, his eyes still locked on to hers. He sighed in relief when at last she responded.

"Tanner, I understand that. I want what you have to offer me. I want to be with you," she assured him. For now, he could go on believing that his ability to give was limited to sexual pleasure, but Natalie was confident he would ultimately be able to embrace the intimacy between them.

Tanner stood, pulling her to him and kissing her with a new passion, a newfound joy that had overtaken him. She was his. His tongue dipped into her sweet mouth and his hand grabbed her tight buttock, squeezing it possessively.

Natalie kissed back with equal fervor, in the arms of the man she craved, the man who was her obsession, her love. Whatever the future held, she knew it would be all right as long as they were together. She arched her back, intentionally pushing her firm ass into his strong hand. *I'm yours—all yours.*

About The Author

Emily Jane Trent writes steamy romances about characters you'll get to know and love. The sex scenes are hot and the romance even hotter! If you are a fan of stories with a heroine that's got spunk and a hunk of a hero that you'd like to take home with you, these stories are what you're looking for. Emily's romantic tales will let you escape into a fantasy – and you won't want it to end - ever.

Dear Reader,

I hope you enjoyed this book. You are the reason I write. Feel free to communicate to me at my blog or on my fan page at Emily Jane Trent Books. Your comments are valuable. I listen. Let's chat.

Warmly,
Emily

Touched By You Series

The romance between Natalie and Tanner unfolds and grows over twelve novellas and I hope you enjoy being a part of their love story.

Read them all?
Sign up for my list and you will be notified of all new releases at www.EmilyJaneTrent.com - just click on the tab "Join Emily's List" – glad to have you.